I0772882

ANGR

Kirk House Publishers

ANGR

BRENT OLSON

ANGR © Copyright 2024 by Brent Olson

All rights reserved. You may not use or reproduce any part of this book in any manner whatsoever without the author's written permission, except for brief quotations included in critical articles and reviews.

The author and the publisher distribute the information in this book on an "as is" basis, without warranty. Even though the author and publisher have taken every precaution in preparing this work, they do not have any liability to any person or entity for any loss or damage caused or alleged to be caused directly or indirectly by the information in this book.

This is a work of fiction. Unless otherwise indicated, all the names, characters, businesses, places, events and incidents in this book are either the product of the author's imagination or used in a fictitious manner. Any resemblance to actual persons, living or dead, or actual events is purely coincidental.

First Printing: September 2024
Second Edition

Paperback ISBN: 978-1-959681-74-8
eBook ISBN: 978-1-959681-75-5
Hardcover ISBN: 978-1-959681-76-2
LCCN: 2024918233

Interior and cover design by Ann Aubitz

Published by Kirk House Publishers
1250 E 115th Street
Burnsville, MN 55337
kirkhousepublishers.com
612-781-2815

ANGER – From the Old Norse word *angr*
Literal translation: *"Grief at the wrongness in the world."*

STILL TRYING

THE SMALL BROWN MAN was on the small brown horse, plodding across the muddy February landscape. The sun shone bleakly through a morning haze. The Coteau Hills across the lake in South Dakota were only faintly visible. Rolling grassland was broken up here and there by the giant rocks that gave Big Stone County its name.

He checked his watch and spoke into the spring air. "I'll call this meeting to order," he said, his body swaying in a gentle rhythm. A voice in his ear trilled, "I'm in the shower. How am I going to keep notes?"

"Maria, you know what time the meeting starts. Besides, you may be the secretary, but you never took notes once in your life. The 'puter does that. You just wanted us to be thinking of you in the shower."

"Maybe. Maybe not. How's the agenda?"

"I'll move we approve it." The voice was deeper, with a faint accent. "We're going to talk about those people from the road, right?"

"Just like always, Sam. Do we have a financial report?"

"Yeah, this is Doug. Ann asked me to give the financial report; she's busy with the kids. As of the first of the month, we have a current balance of $17,342 in cash. In addition, we have 11,700 bushels of corn, 6,500 of wheat, 4,200 of oats. We have nearly 1,000 gallons of apple cider in bulk and 17,280 bottles. Of that, there are almost 3,000 bottles that's either brandy or vinegar by now—Mary Jo was going to tap into some of it next week so we can see where we are. There are 73 large wheels of cheddar, and I think the prosciutto will be ready to eat or sell by the Fourth of July. Seeds for sale—27 varieties of beans with surpluses of ten bushels or more. I didn't put a value on the fruit trees because we're just grafting cuttings onto rootstock per request."

"Did we ever hear back from Rochester?"

"Yeah, they said any medical care we need this year, come on down, it'll be on the house."

"Why so generous?" People were supposed to identify themselves before talking, but in a township with barely a hundred people, most folks didn't see the need.

"Cause we saved their ass. Their turbine went south and they were about to run out of hydrogen for their backup generator. We had the part and we got it to them. That was in December, so we saved some lives. They're not being generous, they're being fair."

"Sam, what we got on Public Defense?"

"Nothing really new." Sam's voice was slow and deep, the words coming out as if each one held individual value. "Those folks who made it here all the way from Belize are settled down by the lake. They say they know aquaculture, and if we'll feed them for six months, they'll be turning out crawfish and have pens built for panfish."

"Is there a motion?"

"What the hell are we doing with those foreigners in our town? We've sent an awful lot of Americans down the road with nothing more than 10 pounds of cornmeal, but you kill the fatted calf for those…Black people." It was another unidentified speaker, but there was a tinge of raw anger in what he said and a hint of a vocabulary he'd chosen not to use.

"Strictly speaking, they aren't strangers." The man's voice was still mild, but there was a tiny hardness creeping in. "The one in charge, he spent one year as an exchange student here when he was in tenth grade, back before the shit. He was a father when the water started rising, he looked around, read the writing on the wall. When the last bit of Belize went underwater, he gathered his family and headed north. Now he's a grandfather and he brought every one of them in safe and sound." His horse shied, feeling the tension in his legs.

He went on, his voice rising and the words running together. "I don't even want to think about what he went through to get them here, and as far as I'm concerned, that's a hell of a résumé. The balls and brains it took to pull that off means I'm not worried about them pulling their weight. And it'll be a cold day in hell before I send them off with nothing." There was a stunned silence when he finished, and he felt a slight embarrassment for the edge in his voice.

"Hey, okay. Calm down. You made the call and we'll back you on it. I move we provide them with a Level Three diet, with milk supplements for the children, for the period of eight months. If they don't pull their weight, we put them on the road again and they can walk to Hudson Bay for all I care."

"I'll second that, but keep my wife away from those kids. If one of them crawls up on her lap once, she'll never agree to putting them on the road."

"Okay, any more discussion? All those in favor?"

It wasn't a unanimous vote, but though not everyone voted "yes," there weren't very many voting "no."

The grass was greening around him, with only a few grimy piles of snow in the shadows of the wind turbines. Perched on the top of a hill, he could see the patchwork of seed plots that provided most of the community's cash income. Angora goats grazed on the last remnants of the leafy spurge that had almost ruined the pastures. He shook his head, remembering the lucky break that had brought the goats to Otrey. With no reliable herbicides available and not enough labor to grub the weeds out by hand, there was less grass every year.

Amy knew a guy who knew a guy who knew a goat rancher in the Black Hills with excess inventory. Nobody had really believed that Angora goats would eat leafy spurge before almost anything else, but it was a measure of their desperation that they sent three guys with a pickup and stock trailer on a thousand-mile round trip with most of their trade goods *and* gasoline. Two weeks later, the goats staggered off the trailer, walked straight to the closest leafy spurge, and started to munch. Twenty years later, they not only had their pastures back, but a new source of income in wool sweaters. He dismounted and opened and closed a gate leading into the Season 6 rotational pasture. The mixed prairie grasses were waist high, even after a winter's weather. The ground squished around his boots, and he knelt long enough to scoop up a handful of mud, kneading it gently into a ball and then working out a small ribbon of dirt, which broke from its own weight when it was only a couple inches long. He smiled. When he was a boy, you could have made pottery out of the clay-rich soil, but now, after decades of work, there was far more organic matter than at any time in the past few centuries"Any other business to be brought before this board at this time?" He paused a moment and then said, "Hearing none, this meeting of the board of Otrey Township, Big Stone County, State of Minnesota, is declared adjourned until next month, date to be determined by when we finish planting wheat."

The green indicator light in his peripheral vision shut off, and he was alone with the springtime. He started to rise to his feet, knees and ankles cracking after a morning on horseback and feeling every day of his 83 years, but one booted foot slipped in the spring mud and he landed on his butt. He let his momentum carry him backward, the damp of the ground coming through his clothes and the chilly blue of the sky giving no warmth. The discomfort was familiar. He'd spent more of his life wet or cold than not, and he felt an urge to remain where he was.

It was a temptation. He wouldn't have to lay here long before he stiffened up, and it wouldn't be long after that before he wouldn't need to worry about ever getting up again. The horse wasn't tied, and he was nearly hidden by the tall grass. Most likely it would be days before anyone found him.

How much longer? I've paid my dues. I've done my share. I'm tired. I'm an old man. I shouldn't still be running meetings and herding cattle—not at my age. I've done my share.

He was in his forties when the first crash came, although there was no way to put an actual date to the slow-motion catastrophe that hit the world. He remembered being cold and hungry, everyone scared, yet holding this place together, cutting loose from the grid and getting all the work done during daylight days or when the wind had the turbines cranking out juice. Shivering by a wood burner that first cold January, weeks at a time when the wind didn't blow and the bitter cold from Canada squatted on the prairie like an evil troll. Catching a deep breath when no one was starving and then the even harder work of convincing the neighbors to return to society, hooking back up to the grid, taking in refugees when they could, working to build the connections that could get you through the hard times. Washington not much help, not even before the tsunami, and not at all afterward.

The memories, dreams, and nightmares rolled behind his eyes, and the dark years, the hard years, reached out and took him away.

SOUTH

A FLAT TIRE IS JUST AN INCONVENIENCE. But if you get a flat tire and you can't find the jack, and the spare is flat, and it's raining, and the guy who stops to pick you up has an ax and anger issues, your flat tire goes from an inconvenience to a horror story. When you study the history of "things going south," that's usually what happens. An inconvenience turns into a problem and then a tragedy.

Sometimes, when a snowball starts rolling downhill, you get an avalanche.

Even though there was already plenty of snow on the mountain, most people would agree that the Houston Barbecue was the snowball that got things started.

In the end, it made no difference, but military investigators and civilian reporters spent six months piecing together what happened on September 11, 2034.

The Antonov AN-26 cargo plane was purchased in Nicaragua for $380,000. Not the perfect plane for the job—beat up, with over 10,000 hours on the airframe, it was a tradeoff between range, capacity, and the ability to land on a rough field.

The CBU-59 cluster bombs were purchased in Pakistan and shipped. The plane could carry 15 of the 800-pound bombs, each of which had 717 smaller bomblets, for a total of over 10,000 different points of explosion and fire. At $3,000 each, plus shipping and handling, the total cost for the munitions was less than $100,000. All in all, only a half-million-dollar investment to sow the wind and reap the whirlwind.

The plane filed a flight plan for Houston but turned east and headed for Texas City. The crew opened the rear cargo door and simply rolled five of the cluster bombs down the ramp and into the air. In twenty minutes, they were over Beaumont, Texas, and another five went out. Fifteen minutes later, the last five went into the air over Lake Charles, Louisiana. The plane landed in a field ten miles west of Welsh, Louisiana. Tire tracks led away from the landing site, but no trace of the crew was ever found. Although the date chosen seemed significant, no terrorist group ever claimed credit. Who knows—it might have been terrorism, or it might have just been a business deal.

Twenty percent of the oil-refining capacity of the United States, along with ports and pipelines, lit up the night sky for three hundred miles. There hadn't been a new refinery built in the United States in forty years, and it was so much easier to cluster refineries in places where the people in charge didn't worry much about zoning. And some people thought that was a good idea.

The fires burned until there was nothing left to burn.

September was a warm month, as was October. By November, some people were cold, and everyone was worried.

But a few had been concerned for years.

BEGINNINGS

JOHN HAD BEEN A FARMER HIS WHOLE LIFE. He left the farm only to attend an agricultural college, where he learned enough accounting to keep books and took a class in business law to keep from getting screwed. When he was asked to learn the Latin names of common weeds, he'd packed up his dorm room and moved back to the farm. There was probably a reason for learning the names, but no one thought to share that reason with him, and he didn't think to share with the people in charge that he thought the class was bullshit. He moved into an empty house a mile from his parents, married the woman he'd loved since they were eight, and went to work. He didn't travel much, and his tolerance for bullshit never improved.

John's formal education stopped at 19, but he read a lot and he noticed everything.

When a coyote got into the chicken pen and took the five laying hens that they'd relied on for breakfast and the occasional angel food cake, he went to Runnings in Milbank to replace them. Standing next to a row of galvanized tubs filled with a variety of chicks, he'd almost pointed out the Leghorns. They were industrial egg layers and nothing else, which is what he thought he needed, but then he'd stood and watched for a while, captivated by the tub that held an assortment of heritage-type chickens for 4-H projects. The breed descriptions were printed on a sheet of paper and in the end, he'd said, "I'll take twenty-five. Give me the Australorp and Ameraucana, maybe some Buffs—something that'll set. And I'll take a couple roosters, too."

He'd never raised chickens to make more chickens, had never seen the need. He'd always been able to rely on someone else, somewhere, making what he needed available. And for some reason, that was starting to feel wrong.

That was definitely the beginning.

If the chickens were the first action he took, the opossums had set the stage. Opossums always seemed like an animal that was little more than the punch line of a joke. Southern animals; he'd never seen one within three hundred miles of his home. Then one year a neighbor thought he saw one, looking like a rat or a raccoon with a naked tail. No one believed him, but next year more people saw them and, in a decade, there were dead ones on the road as often as pheasants. The first one he saw was dead and had a buzzard feeding on it. He was unsettled the rest of the day. Buzzards were new to the area, too.

It had bothered him, seeing the opossums and the buzzards. They weren't where they belonged, and Nature always did things for a reason. When something new showed up on the prairie and prospered, it was because something else had changed. He read as much as anyone, listened to the news, paid attention to the scientists, but he was a man who trusted himself more than he trusted anyone else. He'd watched Al Gore's movie and read the scholarly articles in the Atlantic, but really, it was the opossums and the buzzards that precipitated the chickens.

When his wife got home from work, she went down to look at the new chicks. John watched her walk across the yard, admiring her dark hair and eyes and tiny frame. Even after twenty years, he hadn't tired of her walk, and she often caught him staring at her. When she returned from the chicks, she found him in his office and raised an eyebrow.

"What the hell, John? In the egg business now, are we?"

"Yeah, Amy, I know," John said. "It just seemed like the thing to do. Maybe I'm nuts."

"Maybe you are. You wanna talk about it?"

John laughed. "It's because of Greenland."

"Really? Greenland made you buy five times as many chicks as we need? Well, damn those Eskimos."

"I'm not sure it's completely their fault. No. It just sits there, this big damn island, with ice a couple miles thick all over it, and all that ice is sliding into the sea. Nobody saw it coming, 'cause it takes a long time to melt ice, but the world is warming up and the ice is melting and what the experts really didn't see is that the water on top is running through to the bedrock, and it's lubricating it—like grease in an omelet pan, and all that ice is just gonna slide into the sea."

He brushed one hand across the other, a nervous gesture that showed how upset he was.

"And that means Florida is an island and Bangladesh disappears, and there are a lot of pissed-off or dead people within 50 miles of the coasts all over the world. And pretty much everyone who lives within 500 miles of the Equator is gonna want to be living somewhere else. That's a hell of a lot of people."

He'd started off slowly, but the pace of his words picked up as he accepted what he was saying out loud.

"And it's all happening much faster than anyone thought it would. And that doesn't even take into account all the assholes around the world who blow up the oil fields instead of airliners. We'll be going through all this trauma cold and in the dark and walking. And today I was at coffee in town and everyone's planting corn, and it's all stacked corn on top of it—resistant to Roundup and corn borers, everyone paying God knows what for genetically modified seed that's barely still corn, and everyone seems to think it's all right, good times ahead, no end in sight. I might have the last wheat field in the county, and damned if I can explain to the banker why I do."

"Wow. You're sounding a little tree-huggerish."

"Yeah, I know, and *that* pisses me off. A tree in the wrong place is just another weed. But can't people see that even though we can do something, that doesn't necessarily mean we should? I mean, I'm a believer in penicillin and microwave ovens, but the whole system of commercial agriculture has been doing nothing other than muck about with Mother Nature for the past twenty years. Some of it might not be a good idea. And why should that opinion make me a Commie tree hugger? I mean, is it mandatory that we put our heads in the sand until we get bit on the ass?"

Amy looked at him carefully. "So, bad day today?"

"Well, yeah, maybe a little. Shit, honey, it's just that when I leave this farm or actually even think about the world beyond the grove, my life goes to hell. I can barely drag myself out the driveway anymore."

"So, you bought chickens?"

Maybe it was John who laughed first. Maybe not.

FARM CAMPUS

THE SAINT PAUL CAMPUS of the University of Minnesota was a haven.

Placed on a farm north of the Twin Cities in the 1800s, the city had grown to engulf it, and now it was a half hour's drive from any real farmland. Even in the midst of a major metropolitan area, it had a golf course full of mature oak trees on one side and the empty 320-acre grounds of the Minnesota State Fair on the other. It was a quiet and pleasant location. Except, of course, during the ten days of the Fair. Then it was a freaking nightmare.

The campus no longer felt like a farm, but it was still largely a place for people who wanted to take care of animals and feed the world.

Beth Hendrickson had always loved working there. For the work, but also for the location. It was a short commute down Snelling Avenue, past a good Turkish restaurant and a great Ethiopian one, to her home in the midst of a neighborhood that was as close to quirky as the Twin Cities had to offer. It used to be perfect.

Not anymore. When the wind shifted, the slight tang of smoke from the incinerator turned her stomach, and the empty seat where there shouldn't be one twisted her world and left her shaky and confused.

Her whole life, work had been what saved her, what provided the anchor in troubled seas, and this time she'd tried to bury herself in her work. It wasn't easy at first. She'd be at her desk and whole hours would disappear. Now her work might be going away.

"Explain it to me," the dean said, "as if I were a small child."

Beth desperately tried to choke back her impatience. "As I'm sure you know," she began, "edible beans have a nighttime temperature tolerance of no more than a high of 66 degrees. Above that on a regular basis and the beans don't propagate. We're hitting that threshold more and more. I've had a couple meetings with climatologists and they just look at me like I'm stupid. They see this as just the beginning with no end in sight, and it's happening faster than anyone ever dreamed it would."

"And your research aim is?"

"Okay, there's a bean, native to the Southwest, called the tepary. Nobody grows it anymore, because it's not that good and not very productive. But it does have extraordinary heat tolerance. About twenty years ago, a scientist in Colombia named Alvaro Mejia-Jimenez did some pretty amazing work getting viable seeds from a cross of the tepary and common beans."

"You mean at Columbia."

"No, *in* Colombia, the country. All his research sat on the shelf for a couple decades, but the last few years, people are starting to follow his work and recreate it, with the beans we grow in the Upper Midwest."

"These aren't good times to look for funding for climate change projects. The money isn't there."

"But the need is!" Beth held back her next words. Even people who knew her fairly well could be ignorant of the burning impatience that lurked behind her placid face. She had always known that she lived in a world where something a man would do would be seen as aggressive, but the same behavior from a woman would be seen as hysterical. In defense of getting ahead, she was friendly, helpful, collaborative. She remembered birthdays and anniversaries and never drained the coffeepot in the lounge.

But inside, she burned.

"This is still a land grant university," she said, "and we have a chance to do valuable work that will uphold the reason this university was founded. We can prepare for the future, shed some light in the dark, *save some lives.*"

The dean stared at her for a few moments and then said, "Are you done?" She opened her mouth, then shut it again. "Beth, I know our history and our mission. I also know where money comes from and how much of it there is. And there is a chance, a faint chance, that I know what's possible and what isn't in this world we're living in. Leave your paperwork. I'll take a look at it and see what I can do. In the meantime, teach your classes and try to get along with your peers."

Beth nodded and left, choking back several paragraphs of rebuttals that had occurred to her. She didn't go back to her office but got her car out of the parking lot and got on Cleveland Ave, then Raymond. The drive was slow, but she had plenty of time before school was out. She contemplated stopping at Keys to drown her sorrows in a giant caramel roll and several cups of mediocre coffee but fought down the urge. When she turned the corner toward their house, she saw Steve's pickup parked in the street.

Home early?

"Hey, babe," she said, coming through the door.

"Hey," Steve said, looking up from the dining room table, "how was your day?"

Beth shrugged. "Some days chicken salad, some days chicken shit."

Steve laughed. "You sound like my grandpa when you say that." He watched admiringly as she shrugged off her blazer, dropped her briefcase, and stretched. "But you look nothing like him." She was wearing a silk shell, and without the blazer, she'd gone from professional to…not…in an instant.

"Yeah, well, babe, that's probably best for both you and me." She walked to the dining room window and peered out at her tiny garden. There wasn't much to see. With three children, two working spouses, and one giant bout of depression, gardening took a back seat to almost everything.

"You know," she said, "I've been going to school, one way or another, for twenty years. I have a PhD, years of experience on three continents, and four—*four*—peer-reviewed papers in major publications. But today I was talked to like I was a six-year-old, and kind of a dim, unpleasant one at that."

"No go on the high-temp bean research?"

"No. There's nothing there…I can't really blame Don. I'm not sure how he's keeping the lights on. Plus, the topic…I'm afraid I'm kind of a pariah. But, hey, how come you're home?"

"Yeah, that. I'm heading to North Dakota."

"Now? You can't—you just can't. What will I do?" Beth hated the panicky timbre of her voice. She was on the edge and knew it but loathed feeling weak and afraid.

"If I want to have a job, I go to the airport tonight and head west." There was steel in Steve's voice, very unlike his usual tone. "That was explained to me, clearly. I've been taking a lot of time off."

"You weren't on vacation," Beth snarled. "It's not like we were testing mozzarella in Tuscany."

"I know that. They know that. And they don't care. Nobody cares, Beth. I saddle up or I get left behind, and where am I going to get a job that pays the sort of bills we have?"

"How long will you be gone?"

"No idea. We're checking out fracking sites around Dickinson, and after that, Colorado. Then home. Probably. We're looking at yields, quality, potential…it's going to be a massive report that does who the fuck knows." He shrugged helplessly. "Beth, I'm sorry. I'm an engineer. This is what I do. This is the company I work for. It's time for me to get back to it."

Beth stood with her back to him, looking out the window at the barren garden. "When are you leaving?"

"We're flying to Bismarck tonight. I'm packed. We have to talk about some stuff before we go get the kids."

"I'm not happy about this, Steve."

"Oh, Beth," Steve's voice sagged, "do you think you'll ever be happy?"

The silence lingered, solid and painful.

The plane took off on time. Oddly enough, it was nearly full.

SAVE US

"WHAT'S UP TODAY?" Mornings were almost sedate now after the years spent looking for lost shoes and lunch money. When their baby left for college, they discovered there was time for leisurely breakfasts and date nights. John found the change relaxing and enjoyable, except on the days when he missed it so much he could cry.

"No farming today. Commissioner's meeting. Budget and emergency management."

"Ooooh, sexy."

John looked at her with mild irritation. "Hey, you didn't ask me if what I was doing today made sense; you asked me what I was doing."

"So, about the chickens. Is that all you're going to do?"

John cocked his head. There was a note in his wife's voice he hadn't heard very often, but it was one he never ignored. "Well, I don't know, honey. I'm not convinced a county commissioner from Big Stone County has the authority to reverse global warming. If I do, it wasn't in the handbook. Maybe I could do something about the Middle East. I'll ask the auditor. What exactly do you want me to do?"

"Oh, for Christ's sake, John. You can't save the world. But you can save us—and everyone you know. It's what you do." She stood on tiptoe, bumped noses, and kissed him square on the lips. "It's who you are. Now, get to work."

John stood in the kitchen until the sound of her heels and the scent of her perfume faded and her car left the driveway. He refilled his coffee cup, sat down at his desk, and leaned back in his chair. He linked his hands behind his head for a long moment, staring at the pictures on the wall. Then he scuffed his briefcase from under the desk to check that his agenda, calendar, and a couple of pens were in place. As he opened the top flap, he inhaled the leather smell and ran his hands across the seams, his palms enjoying the texture. He'd bought the briefcase on sale at the Empire Mall in Sioux Falls, right after he'd won his first election for county commissioner. He'd picked it out for no better reason than he'd needed one. It was tan leather, now stained darker in random places from popcorn grease and spilled ink. The handle had broken off within a month, and he'd spliced the shoulder strap twice, but he still liked the smell and saw no need to replace it.

He drummed his fingers briefly on the desk, then picked up his briefcase and went to work.

FIRST MEETING

THE COMMISSIONERS' MEETING was no worse than usual. Four men and one woman—three farmers, an insurance salesman, and a retired banker—worked part time, figuring out ways to keep the roads paved, the least and the lost taken care of, and the county employees from killing each other in interoffice warfare.

Emergency management was the last item on the agenda. The emergency management director worked at it half-time. Harry Swenson by name, his day job was in the county highway department, swapping out bullet-riddled road signs. Ever since 9/11, though, there had been reams of paperwork coming to the county concerning terrorists and securing border crossings. Since the closest border was 250 miles away and the only possible terrorist target was the power plant across the lake in South Dakota, staffing the position hadn't been a real priority. Most of Harry's time was taken up with trying to figure out ways to twist federal antiterrorism grant dollars into something the county could actually use.

"So, Harry," John said, "two questions. I stayed up late last night, reading all this stuff you've given us, and it sounds like we're all ready for a flood, a snowstorm, a grass fire, or a blizzard. What if our emergency is something else?"

"Like what?" Harry asked. "I can't do everything. I have to get ready for what's most likely and what we can handle. Not much sense in preparing for a meteorite or an alien invasion. If something big happens, we'll just have to sit tight, keep our heads, and wait for help to come. If it's a pandemic, I call the public health people. If the Canadians invade, I call the Pentagon."

"And that leads to my second question," John said. "What if no one comes?"

Harry rubbed the bridge of his nose, shuffled his papers into a tidy array, then said, "John, I can't prepare for something that isn't going to happen. If we do have something we can't handle, one phone call and the cavalry will come galloping up. Sure, it might take a few days for the state and feds to get in gear, but we don't really have much choice. We're not mountain men or survivalists; we need an infrastructure and all that goes with it."

Harry took his phone out of its holster and set it on the table. "Look at this. This is what runs our world. Everything that's important has some kind of electronics in it, and there is no one in this county who could do more than change the batteries in it. Hell, it takes a billion-dollar factory just to make these, and then that's all they can make, this one product. Plus, all those factories are 10,000 miles away. Sorry, John, the days of the rugged individualist are gone. Unless you want to live in a cave, you're going to need to depend on everyone else doing their job."

The chairman said, "John, you got anything else? I got hay to bale."

"No, not really. I move we adjourn."

"All those in favor of adjourning, stand up and go home." The chairman whacked the table with his gavel, and the meeting was over.

Harry caught up with John as he was headed down the granite steps outside the courthouse.

"What was that about in there?" he asked. "I didn't understand what you were getting at."

"I don't know, Harry," John said. "Maybe I read too many newspapers. But I think we should put some thought into what if the government gets caught up in a disaster of its own. How are we going to cope out here?"

"I'll tell you how we'll cope. We'll live on cornmeal and bacon, because that's all there'll be to eat in this county within a week if the trucks to the grocery stores don't show up. If there's no electricity, it won't really matter because in the summer the food will be rotten in three days and in the winter, we'll all be froze dead in three days. No sense in making a plan you can't carry out, John. You're just going to have to relax and trust the experts to take care of you."

"You may be right," John said, "but that doesn't mean I don't hate the idea." He walked down the rest of the flight of stairs and then turned around and looked back, squinting into the noon prairie sun. "Besides," he said, "it seems to me that, at least locally, we're the experts, and we haven't the slightest freakin' idea what we're doing. Have you seen any evidence—any in your whole life—that a St. Paul address, let alone Washington, makes a guy smarter than you or me?"

"Don't be telling me that I can relax and let the experts take care of things, because every experience in my life leads me to think that the experts are either self-satisfied dumbasses whose only qualification is that they don't know what they don't know, or else they're guys scrambling in the dark looking for a light switch."

The words tumbled out now—things long left unsaid, but now forming an ugly reality in the air. "Remember the ice storm, Harry? You probably don't, because you were too tired, what with getting that kerosene to your mom in Summit and hauling wood to your in-laws down at the lake so they could stay warm. Where the hell was the cavalry then? Sure, the power companies all sent their trucks and crews and most everyone had juice again in a week, ten days, but that wasn't the government, and the power companies didn't have anything better to do. What if they did? What if the power was out all over? No one's gonna care about us. For Christ's sake, how about

Katrina? One of the biggest cities in the country and no one who mattered did jack shit to help."

"Harry, I'm only one of five people on the board, but you and I both know you took this job because it was the difference between a part-time job with no benefits or a full-time job that gets you health insurance and a pension. I'm giving you a heads-up that you and I, Harry, are gonna take this emergency preparedness serious. It is not just gonna be forms and bullshit."

Harry looked down the stairs. John was not a big man, except through the shoulders and wrists. His hair was thinning and his suit was wrinkled. One hand kept his battered briefcase on his shoulder while the other twirled a set of Chevy keys. But there had been an edge and a force in his voice Harry had never heard before.

"John, I've known you since we were four and you've never talked to me like this before, not ever."

John smiled, then shrugged. "Never had to before." He waved one hand in casual farewell and walked down the block.

DATE NIGHT

JOHN WAS IN HIS RECLINER, laptop across his knees, when Amy got home from work.

"Hey, sweetheart," he said. "What do you know about hydrogen?"

She walked over and kissed the top of his head. He curled an arm around her and squeezed her butt. "That's why I love you. The magic never dies. Yes, I did have a hard day, but I'm glad to be home. And it's soooo nice of you to offer to buy supper. Wasn't it hydrogen that blew up the Hindenburg?"

"Damndest thing," John said. "There's this little island in the North Sea, called Utsira, twenty miles off the coast of Norway. About two hundred people live there and they've got two wind turbines. One just makes electricity and the other uses its electricity to break the seawater down into hydrogen. Then they burn the hydrogen in a generator on days when the wind isn't blowing. And it's been working for years—they've never not had electricity."

Amy was sorting through a handful of mail while he talked. At this, she looked up and said, "That seems complicated. Is it affordable?"

"Well, they do it because it's cheaper than running a cable under the ocean for twenty miles and dragging it up and fixing it every time a shark gets the nibbles. And the thing of it is, how expensive is electricity if it's a choice between expensive and none?"

"Good point. What's for supper?"

"I was thinking I'd take you out. How was work today?"

"Some days, it feels like everyone I work with has serious issues."

"You're a special ed teacher. Everyone you work with does have issues."

"I wasn't talking about the students. They have disabilities. Now, the administration…"

John laughed. "I'll change clothes."

They were sharing a piece of cheesecake when the subject came up again.

"So tell me about your Norwegian island."

"I don't know. I look around here and try to figure out what to do if some mess occurs and we need to look out for ourselves. We've got the best farmland in the world, so we should be able to feed ourselves. Any given time, there's probably a million bushels of corn in the county—that's a lot of corn muffins. That would get us through the first winter, and in the spring, everyone should be able to plant a garden, raise some chickens, something. We need electricity, though. Can't even get a drink of water without electricity. Are you gonna eat that cherry?"

"Yes, I am." She stabbed it preemptively and popped it into her mouth. They were the last customers in the little diner on the edge of Clinton, sitting at a corner table next to a fake fireplace. A faint hum sounded from the fluorescent lights overhead and the big-screen TV was tuned to a game show. The remains of their supper, a beef commercial and fish and chips, huddled on the edge of the table as John drew diagrams with a stubby forefinger on the plastic tablecloth.

"Let's say the average household uses about 5 kilowatt hours a day. We got a couple thousand households in the county. That's about 10,000 kilowatt hours, which means we need about 10 megawatt hours a day to keep all the lights turned on. Seven big wind turbines would do it, except the wind only blows about half the time.

So, what we really need is about twenty wind turbines and some way to store the juice. Now *that's* about fifty million bucks and change."

"John, that's impossible. There aren't fifty million dollars in the whole county," Amy said.

"Well, it's not impossible, but it's going to be a struggle. And that's just the lights. How do we fix broken electronic stuff? What do we do about vitamins and medical care?"

Amy shook her head. "It seems unreal, just talking about it. Are you sure it's necessary?"

"Oh, hell no. I haven't a clue. But think of the thousands of dollars we've spent on life insurance over the years, even though neither one of us planned to die. Remember that documentary about the Holocaust?" He leaned back in his chair and locked his hands behind his head. "Remember that guy who said the Jews all got killed because they owned pianos? It was too much work to move a piano, and too hard to leave it behind, so people just tried to ignore the bad news, because to prepare for the bad times meant thinking about things they didn't want to think about. Well, I think about that." He leaned forward and took a drink of water, then looked into her eyes. "I think about that all the time."

He glanced at the check, pulled a twenty out of his wallet, and left it next to his plate. On the way out, he held the door for his wife, taking the opportunity to study her backside as she walked by. Feeling the gaze, she gave a little wiggle on her way to the car.

The ride home was almost silent—the sun set behind them and the nightly obstacle course of deer, pheasants, and skunks on the road. Their mailbox was in view when Amy spoke again.

"So, we going to do this?"

"Oh, shit, honey, I'm afraid so." John reached across the car and held her hand, his thumb rubbing her wedding band. "What's the first step?"

"I think I'm going to talk to Bobby."

She retrieved her hand and leaned back against the door. "I suppose that makes sense," she said, "but you're going alone."

"Sweetheart, I wouldn't have it any other way."

BOBBY

IT WAS A WEEK BEFORE John found time to go see Bobby. As he drove with the window open, the hot August wind swirled dust behind the pickup, and a bead of sweat trickled through his chest hair. His fingers tapped a gentle tattoo on the windowsill, and his T-shirt clung damply to the small of his back. "The River" 97.3 was on, and an old John Mellencamp song about small towns played above the road noise.

Bobby's driveway was a quarter mile long. Two shallow trenches were worn in the gravel, with grass and weeds growing in the middle. It disappeared into the middle of a straggly grove of box elders and wild plum. In the center of the grove, an old farmhouse squatted. Most of the house was covered with battered cedar siding, but there were two ramshackle porches covered with wide Masonite siding, the paint peeling off in tattered strips. The lawn was grown three feet high, with paths worn through to the front door and to a chicken house. Random hunks of old machinery poked up like reefs in an ocean. John frowned as he saw a broken attic window with plastic stapled across it and faded yellow insulation stuffed in the cracks.

The driveway circled around the house, and John parked on the far side. In the deep shade, he saw a rusty wrought-iron table, a few chairs, and a sagging hammock. John got out of his pickup and picked his way through the undergrowth toward the hammock. A dusty Cadillac Escalade sat in the shade, covered with bird droppings and sporting a bumper sticker that proclaimed, "Pop Country Sucks!" It leaned into the shade with one flat tire.

John gazed without pleasure at the figure in the hammock. "You've got a flat tire," he said.

"No, not me, I'm fine," came a sun-dazed reply. "I've got a spare tire. My car, now that's got a flat tire." Bobby rolled over on his back and opened his eyes.

"Oh, shit," he said, falling out of the hammock and scrambling to his feet. "John," he said, his arms outstretched and waving, "I was really drunk. I had no idea what I was doing." Bobby had a significant paunch stretching out a Slobberbone T-shirt, unkempt blonde hair, and flip-flops stuck on the end of a pair of pale, hairy legs. A pair of black-framed glasses sat askew on his face.

John sighed. "You dummy. What the hell were you thinking, putting your hand on my wife's ass? I see the black eye has gone away—are you aware just how fortunate you are? You're lucky the only thing she could reach was a jar of salsa. If there'd been a brick on the table, you'd probably be dead."

"I said I was sorry. I was drunk."

"You say that like it's some sort of excuse. If drinking makes you stupid, you should do less of it."

"We've had this talk before," Bobby said cautiously.

"Well, yeah. Seems like the first time was in eighth grade. You didn't listen then, haven't listened since, so I'm thinking of tapering off on that topic for a couple of decades." John glared at a cocklebur plant and pulled it up by the roots. "I've got something else I want to talk about. What are we going to do if the end of the world is coming?"

"I suppose 'get drunk' is the wrong answer?"

"Yeah, not so much. You got any coffee in that house? We could be here a while."

"Are we okay? You know, you scared the shit out of me, showing up now."

"Why?"

Bobby stared intently through smeared lenses, his head tilted and his body tense. "Well, 'cause if you'd shown up here that next morning, mad, I figured you'd just punch me out. But that party was two weeks ago. If you'd calmed down and still come over, I, uhhh, didn't want to be here."

John sighed, "Jesus, Bobby. Shut up and get your ass in the house and make us a pot of coffee. I got no time to be dealing with remorseful drunks. You got a black eye, and my wife thinks you're a jackass. That seems like enough punishment for one day."

Bobby led the way up the sidewalk, a row of uneven cement stepping stones set into the grass. A huge black tomcat with one missing ear and a crooked tail crouched in the doorway and meowed for entry. Bobby picked him up and held him in the air by both cheeks. "You big dope." "All you had to do was not crap in the house. That was the deal—don't crap in the house and you'll be happier than any tomcat you know. It's your own damned fault." He set the cat down and nudged him out of the way with one foot. It snarled, slapped at his foot, and slunk balefully to the shady side of the house.

◆　◆　◆

The inside of the house was as disordered as the yard. Stacks of magazines and books defined narrow paths through the rooms, and piles of discarded clothes grew in the corners.

John sniffed the air. "You said you were going to get rid of the cats."

"Yeah, I did. It just, you know, I haven't had time to clean up."

"Your mamma would disapprove of what you've done with the place."

Bobby looked perplexed. "I haven't done anything to it. It's been the same since the day she died."

"Yeah, I know. But that was twenty years ago. Some people clean house once a decade or so. This place is a sty."

"Hey!" Bobby said. "Enough, okay? What did you want, any-way?"

John swept a pile of magazines off the seat of a tattered velour easy chair and plopped down.

"Do you worry about opossums?"

MASLOW KNOWS

"OKAY," BOBBY SAID, "are you familiar with Maslow's Hierarchy of Needs?"

He was sprawled in a massive leather recliner, a new notebook computer in his lap. He threw a piece of popcorn into the air, tried to catch it in his mouth. When it bounced off his chin and dribbled onto the floor next to an empty beer bottle and a pizza box, he ignored it and began to talk again.

"Back in the forties, a dude named Maslow said humans have a variety of needs, and he ranked them in importance. Like the bottom layer is air, food, water, sex, and sleep. The higher you go on the pyramid, you go from physiological needs to safety, then love, then a bunch of touchy-feely crapola toward the top. Personally, I think it's all bullshit. I'm more of a believer in Manfred Max-Neef's theory about fundamental human needs. He's an economist from Chile who says people all have the same needs—like food, protection, affection, and a bunch of others I can't remember."

He paused and pointed a finger in the air. "The important thing to remember is that folks are complicated. So, you might think that food, clothing, and shelter are all you need to worry about, when in fact you need medical care, education, and beyond that, people need to feel like they're contributing and like they can improve their lot in life. And, since this is America, no matter what you do, people need to feel like they were part of the decision, or else no one is gonna do what you say. And, of course, you've got the whole

Tersky/Kahneman behavioral economics theory to muddle everything up.”

“All I want to do is keep the lights on, Bobby. I’m not interested in doing group therapy or singing Kumbaya around a campfire.”

John paced up and down the narrow room, punting a half-empty bag of dill pickle potato chips out of his way. He looked down at Bobby and his laptop. “What is that thing, anyway?”

“Doesn’t really have a name. I had a guy make it for me.

“Jesus, Bobby, haven’t you heard of Amazon? What’s it cost to have someone build you a laptop?”

“A lot. But I could run the world with it. If I, you know, wanted to.”

“And if you were offered the job. No offense, but it’s hard to see that happening. Although, truthfully, Bobby, I don’t see how you could do any worse.”

“Thanks. But you’re wrong about the sitting around a campfire singing Kumbaya. There are lots of places in the world that have all kinds of resources but are still crappy places to live. Look at Russia—based just on available, exploitable natural resources, it should be a freakin’ paradise, but instead the national slogan is ‘Fucked up for 1,000 Years.’ You need stuff, but you also need something that ties you together as a community instead of a bunch of people just squabbling over who gets the biggest piece of pie. After WWII, Germany was just a pile of burning bricks, but look at it now. On the other hand, Afghanistan hasn’t cleaned out their irrigation ditches since Genghis Khan scuffed some mud into them. Germany’s a real country, Afghanistan isn’t. You gotta think about shit like that.”

John got up and straightened a crooked picture on the wall. “Things are going to hell. I can *feel* it, and nobody seems to know their ass from a hole in the ground. I wish I hadn’t run for county commissioner. Then all this would be someone else’s business.”

“I told you not to. I told you it would be a pain in the ass. But if I remember right, you needed the money and the health insurance.

And, all due respect, Mr. Commissioner, but you're talking bullshit. In case you haven't noticed, this really *isn't* your business. We've got a president, Congress, a governor—all sorts of people in nice suits who are getting paid good money to pay attention to shit like this. You're just supposed to keep the roads paved and fight off the DNR from buying the whole county and turning it into a duck refuge. That's all your constituents want you to do."

He stretched in his recliner, wiggled his toes, and rubbed his eyes. Leaning back, with his eyes closed and hands behind his head, he said, "But, John, where the real bullshit comes in is you saying you wish this was someone else's problem. You forget, I know you. In kindergarten, you were telling people the most efficient way to line up for milk break. You've spent your whole life choking back the urge to scream, 'Let me do it for Christ's sake!' But since you're a nobody from a nowhere place, you can't fix everything. But you and me, Johnny, we can fix this place. You and me—I'll be the brains behind the scene, and you can be the charming politician who gets people moving."

John stopped pacing.

"Terrific. You the brains and me the charm. I'm as charming as a turnip, and you're a drunken moron."

Bobby brandished his laptop above his head. "Wonders of technology, my friend. I don't have to know anything—I just have to know it's out there and I can go find it. You, on the other hand, really do have the charm of a turnip. You better work on that."

"You want a drink?" He stood up and headed for the kitchen.

John said, "It's 11:00 a.m. on a Wednesday, I got about a gazillion things to do. Amy thinks I'm nuts for even coming over here, and you want to get boozy?"

"Just a bump to get the day rolling. I got cheap tequila or some beer handmade in a thousand-year-old monastery by Belgian monks wearing wool robes handed down for five hundred years."

"Yeah, that sounds sanitary. Do monks sweat? I'll take the te-quila."

BUMBLEBEE

THREE HOURS LATER, John tripped on a loose board coming out of the house. He caught his balance and shut the door as Bobby's snores reverberated behind him.

"Oh, hell," he said. "Bobby, I'm a DWI poster child. That's going to look good in the paper." His head spinning, he stumbled down the sidewalk and slid to the ground, his back against a giant ash tree. The bark was rough against his skin, the air around him still and humid. A bumblebee caught his eye as it lurched from flower to flower.

"You look like you better not drive either, partner."

John thumped his head against the tree and looked up toward the cloudless sky. Was this going to work? Should it work? Was it necessary? Just because Bobby had signed on didn't really mean this was a good idea—Bobby would sign on for a bus trip to Patagonia if he thought there'd be good beer and pork rinds on board.

John rubbed his hands together, then picked at a loose callus and examined a blister.

What the hell do I know, anyway? Just a farmer who never finished college, never left home, and works part-time running the smallest, poorest county in the state. There's a whole world of experts out there who surely would be hard at work fixing things if things were really wrong.

He studied the bumblebee again. He'd heard somewhere that a so-called expert had written a mathematical proof that a bumblebee couldn't fly. Experts like the doctor who'd told his mom she would beat the cancer, experts like the marketing people who'd told him when to sell his grain, experts who'd told him when to buy land and had shrugged their shoulders and talked about paradigm shifts when the bottom fell out of the land market, experts like all the smart asses who wore nice suits and talked down to guys with chipped fingernails and sore backs.

He sighed and rubbed the heels of his hands against his eyes. When his vision cleared, he focused on the flat right rear tire on Bobby's Escalade. He struggled to his feet and sought out the spare. Just sliding the jack under the rear axle was enough to break a sweat. By the time he had the tire changed, his shirt was soaked and his head had cleared enough to drive. As he stretched the kinks out of his back, he saw the bumblebee again.

"You and me, bee, you and me."

And then he went home.

HARNESS THE WIND

JOHN PAUSED AT THE FIRST GRANITE STEP leading up to the courthouse. The old brick building towered over him. He gazed without favor at the edifice, his eyes wandering from the tiled roof to the troublesome downspouts, to the bricks he knew would need to be tuck-pointed in another five to seven years. He spared a frown for a sidewalk that had been replaced three years ago but already showed signs of cracking. A glance at his watch told him the meeting started in ten minutes. As he climbed the steps, he ran his hand along the iron railing and glared at the small flecks of black paint speckling his hand.

He was slightly out of breath when he walked into the board room and flung his briefcase on the conference table.

It was a small room, barely big enough for the table and a few visitor chairs. The table was chipped, but the chairs were comfortable. An American flag stood in the corner, and a map of the county highlighted drainage ditches and roads. The chairman, a hog farmer from the north end of the county named Alan Thompson, plopped himself down next to John. His knuckles were scarred, and a faint odor of manure and disinfectant hovered around him. "Hey!" he said to the room, "Do you know why Star Trek and toilet paper are alike? They both go around Uranus, wiping out Klingons." He laughed, but mostly alone. John faked a smile and a chuckle.

The county had skimmed by on three potential harassment suits in the past three years, and as John smiled, he vowed that the next time one came up, Thompson was just going to be left hanging. John poured himself a cup of bad coffee, stood up for the Pledge of Allegiance, and then spent most of the meeting drawing three-dimensional boxes, with an occasional foray into tents and faces, on the edge of his agenda.

"Any more business?" the chairman asked, his gavel wavering in the air.

"Yeah," John said, "couple things. First, I see a couple tiles are missing on the roof—just north of the skylight. We better get them fixed or we'll have falling plaster again. And the railing needs to be painted."

"Next," he said, "I think the county needs a windmill. Maybe a bunch of 'em."

"What the hell, John?" Alan said. "Are you nucking futs? How is that our business?"

"Why not? Our job is to take care of the people in this county. We need money to do that; we get money from taxes. Everybody already pays too many taxes. Look at our demographics—we've got 5,000 people, most of them old, many of them uneducated, and we're two hundred miles from the Cities. All we've got is the wind. Let's use what we got."

John went on, talking faster. "Now, Henry took early retirement. Mary says with the new computer system she doesn't need to replace him, so that's fifty grand in the budget that we're not going to use. Let's funnel that into the economic development fund, hire some guy to do the groundwork and get a bunch of windmills going. I don't care who owns them or who profits—we still get the tax money and a few people get jobs. Every windmill in the county is another $2,500 in tax revenue, every year, forever. What the hell? Whatta we got to lose?"

He winked at Alan. "C'mon—you're up for re-election next year, and you live in the best part of the county for wind turbines. You tell your constituents that you've saved them 50 grand a year on property taxes, they'll carry you to the courthouse on their shoulders."

Alan gave him a long look, then said, "Did I tell you about my car accident? Just a little fender bender, but I get out of my car and the other guy gets out of his car and he comes walking back to me, and he's a no-shit dwarf. He looks at his car and looks up at me and says, 'I'm not happy!' and I says, 'Well, which one are you then?'" He threw his head back and laughed, pleased beyond all measure. Then he leaned over and whispered to John, "You pull this off, and I'll be happy."

The vote was 5–0, and there was one check mark on John's list.

BACK TO BOBBY

JOHN TOOK HIS PHONE AWAY from his ear, held it against his stomach, and called out, "Amy, darlin', sweetheart…"

"No. The answer is no." Her voice came from the kitchen.

"You haven't heard the question yet."

"I don't need to. When you get that disgusting little whine in your voice, I'm pretty sure I'm not going to want to hear what comes next."

"Well, you're maybe right. I want you to come with me to Bobby's tonight. I need to talk to him, and I want your opinion on whether or not he's making sense."

"Oh, John." Amy growled deep in her throat, then said, "Okay. But you better give him a heads up that I'm not in the mood for any crap of any kind."

"Got it. I think even Bobby is capable of learning from experience. Just bring a jar of salsa and toss it up and down."

John could almost hear her blush. "Don't think I won't do it. And you're buying me supper after."

John laughed and spoke into the phone, "We'll be over in a couple hours. You could maybe try and spiff up the joint a bit, just for the heck of it."

Daylight showed through a couple more bullet holes in Bobby's mailbox, but otherwise things looked about the same. John stopped the pickup in the bend of the driveway. The tall grass in the yard was starting to dry out and lean over, with a few scattered, stalwart burdock bushes standing head high and five feet in diameter.

Amy said, "Just for the record, why, exactly, are we here?"

John stared out the windshield, fingers drumming on the steering wheel and not making eye contact. "A few reasons. Bobby's smarter'n hell—he knows stuff we don't. But he also doesn't know what he don't know, which can be a problem. You're here for the common sense. And, uh," a slow flush started on the back of his neck as he paused for breath, "Amy, I don't have a lot of friends." Amy tipped her head slightly, her eyes widening in concentration. John kept staring straight ahead. "You're one, and Bobby's another, and that's about it. I'm feeling the need for some friends." He turned to meet her gaze and shrugged apologetically, almost wincing, then he popped open the pickup door and started toward the house. Amy followed a few seconds later.

Bobby met them halfway down the sidewalk. He was dressed in a clean, wrinkled white shirt and blue jeans, his sockless feet jammed halfway into moccasins.

"Hi!" he said brightly. "Come on in." He led them up the sidewalk. The black cat was in front of the door, and as they approached, he stood up and curled around Bobby's ankles, meowing. Bobby picked him up by the cheeks and held him, eye to eye. "I told you, all I ask is, 'Don't crap on the bed.' How hard is that? Cats all over the world, happy cats, successful cats, use litter boxes. So, don't whine at me." The cat writhed frantically. As Bobby set it down, it bit him on the thumb and darted around the corner. Bobby licked the blood off his hand and waved them through the door. John looked around. The house looked a lot better, and smelled a little better. The actual garbage was off the floor, and the books and magazines were neatly stacked in corners. Amy walked warily into the room and suppressed a sniff at the lingering odor of tomcat.

Bobby said, "Before we go any further, Amy, I'd like to apologize for what happened. I was wrong, and I'm sorry."

Amy looked at him and gave a short nod.

Bobby went on, encouraged. "Actually, you know, in a way it was kind of a compliment."

Ohhhh, shit, John thought.

Amy had started to sink down into a straight-backed chair, but this brought her to her feet and across the room. She was much shorter than Bobby, but with her head tilted back and both fists on her hips, she seemed even shorter as she stood toe to toe.

"No, it wasn't, Bobby! No, it wasn't! How stupid are you! What the *hell* were you thinking? Is that what you see when you look at me? Do I *look* like the sort of woman who'd let some worthless drunk paw her at a party? I've known you since second grade. Have I *ever* given you any reason to think that's who I am?"

"Amy," John said mildly, stepping to her side. "Please don't hit him. If you hit him, then I'm going to have to hit him, and then the day is shot to hell for all of us. If Bobby promises to shut up about this, forever, can we get on with why we're here?"

Bobby opened his mouth, but with a glance at John, he shut it again. Amy took a deep breath and returned to her chair. John looked both ways and then began.

"Okay," he said, "I got fifty grand from the board for windmill stuff—zoning, research, stuff like that. It looks like with the new mandates, if we give the utilities some sort of deal on taxes through the county, somebody's going to put up some windmills here. What's next?"

Bobby said, "I've been thinking about this a lot. Let's say we can keep the lights on. Next is food—the whole place is full of farmers. They can learn how to grow crops other than corn and beans. Those two are easy."

"When do the hard ones come in?" Amy asked.

"What if we pull it off? What if things go to hell, but right here the lights are on and there's food on the table. Why don't we just paint a freakin' bulls-eye on our foreheads? If we're surrounded by hungry, cold, scared people, they're going to want to come here. I mean, what the hell are they going to do in Woodbury or Edina? They won't go east because Wisconsin is going to fill up with folks running away from Chicago. They won't go north because it's cold and you can't eat pine trees, and they won't go south because what idiot would want to live in Iowa?"

Bobby kicked back in his recliner, pulled the laptop out from under the couch, and brought up Google Earth. "Let's say something happens. The Greenland ice cap melts and raises the ocean twenty feet. Hoof-and-mouth disease breaks out and we have to kill every cow in America. Terrorists blow up any of a gazillion things that could bring society crashing to a halt: some guy with a cough gets on a plane in Zaire and a month later we've got twenty million people dead of Ebola or the like. Doesn't matter what happens, just picture the book of Revelations."

"Now, we're two hundred miles from the Cities. The meek and the mild, the dumb and lazy ones are going to die right there, without moving a muscle. You'd find their withered little corpses in their houses or condos, ears straining to hear 'CCO,' waiting for the governor to say something smart. We all know how long a wait that's going to be."

Bobby looked down and drummed his fingers on the cover of the laptop. "No. Here's the thing. The ones who will make it out here are going to be the best and the worst. And it might be damn hard to tell the difference." Bobby paused for emphasis. His voice went dark.

"We're really going to want to keep this on the down low. We're not going to want a bunch of people to think this is the place to go. And that's just the beginning. Johnny, I'm afraid we're going to have to get some guns."

"There are 5,000 people in Big Stone County," John said. "I bet there are 6,000 guns. We already have way more guns than we have people I trust with guns."

◆ ◆ ◆

Bobby belched with joy. The battery on his laptop had given out an hour ago, and now he was using it for a coaster. Chips and salsa smeared the lid, soon to be joined by brown-colored drips as Bobby waved his bottle of Kasteel Brown.

"No, no, no," he said. "What we should do is set you up as some sort of earl or duke, running the county on your own authority. You're an elected official—that gives you an in to take on more authority. Then the sheriff, the militia, and everyone will report to you. And the whole thing will just evolve from there. That's the way the world has run for thousands of years—one guy on top, everyone else toeing the line."

"Jesus, Bobby," John said, "that's the dumbest thing I ever heard. It sounds like a movie, and that's why it won't work. Most movies are stupid—you know, all the cop shows where the maverick with the heart of gold or the lovable screw-up solves the case. You know why that is? 'Cause everyone in Hollywood is a screw-up, especially the writers, and screw-ups like to think that if the world changed just a tiny bit, they'd be the ones in charge. But do you know what screw-ups do? They screw things up!"

He paced around the room, violently scratching his head with both hands. "Jesus, Bobby, you're a grownup, you've lived a while. Tell me one time, one time, when some goofball, some shootin'-from-the-hip, damn-the-Man, make-it-up-as-we-go-along dumbass, actually got anything done?"

"No, it's always the boring guys, the guys who check the math, who put air in the tires, who pay the bills on time. You go the other way, you get Custer at the Little Bighorn, yelling 'Charge' right into the whole Sioux Nation. So when you start talking about shit like the Duchy of Big Stone, it makes my brain hurt, 'cause it's a screwball idea."

50

He stopped walking and pointed a finger at Bobby. "No, I see three things happening. One, the people who were in charge will still be in charge. Some people are leaders, some aren't and that's just the way the world is. Two, *nobody* will be in charge; we'll all just muddle along on our own as best we can. It'll be dog eat dog and lock your doors at night." He shook his head at the prospect and gazed into the distance.

"What's third?" Amy asked.

"Third is the bad one. Some absolutely ruthless son of a bitch will take over, 'cause he'll be willing to do what no one else will even consider. Think Stalin, or Idi Amin, or any of another hundred ruthless sons of bitches. And he'll get a hold of the guns from the Armory, and he'll turn the high school into his castle and he'll have a harem and minions and everything else that sounds like it comes from a bad novel, but it's all happened before, all around the world. And after a while someone will catch him on a bad day and whack off his head and it'll all start over, except with less of everything, and maybe in a hundred years or so something good might turn up. But that isn't a sure thing. It'd be just as likely that we'd have 500 years of Dark Ages."

He stopped in front of Bobby's recliner and waggled a forefinger at him. "So, Bobby, there will be no Duke of Big Stone. We're not even going to talk about it. Let's concentrate on not starving in the dark, okay? That'll be a great plenty to get done; we pull that off and we'll be able to call it a day. Okay?"

Bobby waved his beer bottle and belched again. "Okay," he said, "okay. I get it. But I don't think you're giving the idea a fair chance. I didn't even have time to explain how I'd be the power behind the throne. Like Cardinal Richelieu in The Three Musketeers. Maybe I could even wear robes."

"Jesus, Bobby. Shoes," Amy said. "Why don't you start with shoes and work up from there. Robes can come later."

"You got it, Amy," Bobby said enthusiastically, "anything for you. Hell, socks might not even be out of the question."

Amy stood up and walked toward the door. On her way, she paused to pat Bobby's shoulder. "Don't go crazy there, Bobby. One step at a time. Although I do appreciate the effort. John, can we go home? I've got things to do."

"Yeah, okay," John said. "Bobby, we're out of here. Thanks for the beer. And Bobby?"

Bobby tipped his head back and looked him in the eye.

"Lights and food, Bobby, lights and food. One step at a time. And keep in mind we are not using anything that ever came out of Hollywood or *any* science fiction book you've ever read for a guide. Got it?"

Bobby smiled forlornly. "I coulda been a prince."

John shrugged. "That's right. You could have been a prince. But you're not, and that's a choice you made a long time ago."

LOSING GROUND

JOHN SLIPPED ON THE SIDEWALK and did a frantic mid-air shuffle, getting his feet under him and barely avoiding a tumble into an icy hedge.

Alan Thompson was coming up behind him and laughed out loud. "Johnny, I had no idea you were so graceful. You looked like a ballerina there. Hey, that reminds me, did you hear about the woman in a sundress who walks into a bar…"

"Yeah, yeah, yeah," John's voice overrode his, "Any woman can kick that high, she's a ballerina as far as I'm concerned."

Alan laughed, "Helluva joke, idn't it?" He reached out a hand and helped John regain his balance. "Hey, you're looking a little glum. What's up? Life is good."

"Yeah, it is for you," John said. "You just got reelected. Four more years before the taxpayers figure things out and can give you the boot. Me, I'm going to be running when all the bills come due."

"It's your own damn fault, John. Those wind turbines do look pretty, but it was your idea to give them a tax break."

"Well, the tax abatement was a deal killer. No break, no turbines. I do believe in the long run it's going to be for the best."

"Who the hell cares about the long run? You told everyone that if they put up with a bunch of wind turbines on the skyline, their taxes were going to go down. Now, they got the turbines and their taxes are going up. You think nobody's going to notice? Just between you and me, John, you should know by now that nobody—

not me, certainly not the voters—really cares about the long run. Tell 'em what you're gonna do for them tomorrow; that's really all that matters."

Alan stopped walking long enough to scoop up a gum wrapper off the sidewalk and glare at it. "That goddamn janitor is slacking off again. Does anyone at this freakin' courthouse actually work for a living? No, the taxpayer don't care about the long term, and can you blame him? The average guy in this county has to pay his bills tomorrow, help put his kids through school, spend some money to keep the old lady happy, and it's all gotta happen right now." Alan stopped again, one foot on the bottom step leading up to the court-house door.

"John, let me tell you. You keep going on and on about the environment this and that—you're gonna be gone next election. This tree-hugger shit isn't gonna fly, not out here. That only works in places where people have enough money that they can afford to care."

Alan clapped him on the shoulder. "John, I'd hate to lose you, but I don't see where you're coming from with some of this stuff. People need lower taxes and better jobs. They need to know the roads are kept up and the sheriff's busting drug dealers and only giving speeding tickets to folks from out of town. They don't want the DNR buying any more farmland, and they don't want welfare creeps moving out here from the Cities. That's it. Anything else is just a frill, and we can't afford frills."

"But what if I'm right, Alan?" John asked. "What if I'm right?"

"Doesn't matter," Alan said. He was halfway up the steps, and John was talking to the back of his knees. "Jesus, John, it don't matter. We can't fix it, we can't make it stop, and it probably ain't gonna happen anyway. Just shut up about your theories or you're gonna be looking for a real job."

John followed him up the stairs and hit another patch of ice. His right leg went up, his arms windmilled frantically, and he spread-eagled on the ground.

Alan looked back, laughed, and said, "Johnny, you look like you're getting nailed to the cross." He opened the door of the courthouse and looked down the hall. "Where is that goddamn janitor?"

POKE ME

"NO, NO, NO," BOBBY SAID. He was back in his recliner, a Minnesota January faintly visible through the fogged windows of his living room. He was wearing slippers, grey sweatpants, and a stained cashmere bathrobe. "Poke me, baby." He held out a coffee cup of spiced wine. John reached into the fieldstone fireplace and pulled out an iron poker, the tip glowing red hot. He walked across the room and gently stirred the wine with it. Steam rose and Bobby sniffed deeply. "God, I love winter," he said. "There are just so many good winter drinks. In the summer you got vodka tonics and beer, maybe a Moscow Mule, and that's about it. Winter, the sky's the limit."

"Yeah, well, the sky's the limit if you got someone to wait on you hand and foot," John said. "What are you 'no, no, noing'?"

"Not everyone can heat their houses with wood. This is the prairie. Not that much wood around, and how about schools and hospitals and stuff. Can you imagine how much wood it would take to heat the high school? I don't even know if you could find a wood burner that big. No, it won't work. You've got to work with what you got. Now, if we were starting a town from scratch, we could just bury it in the south slopes near the lake. Get a house underground, with good, big windows, and you can heat it with a candle and cool it with an ice cube. But we don't have that. What we have is a county where half the housing is 80-year-old two-story houses with crappy windows, not enough insulation, and propane and natural gas furnaces. No, we'll have to go with hydrogen."

"Hydrogen? How do you convert a propane furnace to burn hydrogen?"

"Shit, I don't know. But I know people who know, and that's even better. No, Johnny, I've been thinking about it a lot, and with a lot of this stuff we're just pissing into the wind, because when you look at our infrastructure, we need some sort of liquid fuel to make things work. If things go to hell, the only fuel we can get, we'll have to make. Now, you can talk pyrolysis. That's where you heat a bunch of grass up to a gazillion degrees and it turns into low-grade fuel oil. That works, but it's hard on equipment and it's complicated to use. A better idea might be gas from algae, except that seems gross to me. Hydrogen would be like running a propane tractor. They'd run forever, and the oil would stay clean and the plugs would look like new. There are lots of ways to make hydrogen."

"Yeah, expensive ways."

"We don't care! Geez, we're saving the world here. You asked me to help you prepare for a freakin' catastrophe. Okay, we get a freakin' catastrophe and money won't matter. Do you think people are going to care if it costs 8 cents a kilowatt or 18, if the choice is between lights and no lights? Hell no, they'll say, 'Hook me up.'" He waved his cup in the air enthusiastically, spilling a little wine onto the lapel of his robe. "Hook me up," he repeated, "that's all they'll say."

"Maybe," John said, "but right now, all I have is people asking me how much it's going to cost. If I'm going to keep my job, I have to be able to tell people something that makes sense."

"Oh, John," Bobby said, pushing his glasses up and locking eyes across the room. "You're going to lose your job. You know that, don't you? Hell, I'm just hoping to keep you out of jail, and that isn't even a sure thing. You are definitely going to lose your job."

"Yeah," John said. He walked to the window, placed his palm against the frost for a moment, then wiped the area clean. He peered out into the storm and said, "Yeah, I know I'm going to lose my job. But I don't think Amy knows, so try and keep your mouth shut about it."

"Geez, John," Bobby said, "Amy's smarter than the both of us put together. I bet she knew a year ago."

"Well then, let's just leave that as something we both know but don't talk about. I've found that's the secret of a good marriage: not talking about what isn't going to change. You want some more wine?"

Bobby held out his cup. "Poke me, baby."

"Wouldn't it be simpler to just put in the microwave?"

"Ambience, baby, ambience. Plus, you're already up."

SAVING THE PROFESSOR

THE GAVEL CRASHED.

John said, "I call this meeting of, ahh, the Five County Higher Education Facilitation and Enhancement Committee to order."

After the usual nonsense of minutes, agendas, and notices, the real business began. The chancellor of the University of Minnesota, Morris, was first to speak.

"Gentlemen," she said. She wore a black dress, with a slender gold chain around her neck. "As you no doubt know, there have been some rather dramatic funding cuts for the University of Minnesota system, due to continuing budget deficits at the state level. One of the more unfortunate results of those cuts is that the administration has decided to prioritize their research dollars at the Twin Cities campuses. Now, UMM has been an integral part of this community and this area for over half a century. We've contributed jobs and cultural enrichment, and now, we're asking for your help." She paused for a breath, and John interrupted her.

"Just what sort of help are we talking here?"

"If you don't mind, perhaps it would be best if I could give some information to set the scene for our request. I have a short Power-Point, which we feel provides some valuable background and enables a more comprehensive feel for what we have in mind."

"Thank you, Doctor," John said, "but why don't you just tell us what you want, and we can fill in the blanks ourselves. If we have any questions, then we can start delving deeper. I mean, it's the middle of April. There should be some sort of constitutional amendment about having to listen to a PowerPoint on a beautiful spring day." He smiled to lower the sting, but it wasn't a sincere smile.

There were a few muffled chuckles, and the chancellor might have blushed a little. "That's fine. To make a long story short, we need $150,000 a year for the next four years in order to keep a potentially revolutionary program functioning."

"That's a lot of money, Professor." It was a commissioner from Traverse County, a man in his midseventies with a bullet head and a crew cut. "Our people are paying too much money in taxes already. Why in the world should we ask them to support something that won't help them a bit?"

"Because it will," the chancellor said. "We have a terrific young professor and a core of students who are building a program around a self-sustaining colony on Mars. We're talking nanotechnology computers, foam batteries where the charging matrix can be made from products as mundane as wood pulp, with a substrate of easily available copper—just so many miraculous products where the basic research is already done; we just need to fit it all together."

The commissioner from Traverse spoke again, "This isn't Mars. Why in the world would I want to commit a dime to something that doesn't affect my constituents at all? If this is the greatest thing since sliced bread, why won't someone else fund it?"

The chancellor shrugged. "The catch is the cost. This is all expensive, which is why we've structured the program around a colony where cost is not as big a factor as it is for an industry committing funds to build a half-billion-dollar factory. There are so many good ideas out there, and the industry is afraid to commit until a clear winner rises up. Think VHS tapes vs. Betamax. We've done it on a small scale, but so far we have not managed to devise a way to scale up the process and keep the production costs anywhere near current technology. Frankly, the industry is moving in a different direction, but we still feel there are avenues left unexplored. If we are correct, there will be no need for billion-dollar chip factories scattered along the Pacific Rim—computers can be almost a cottage industry, with production on a small, highly personalized scale. We can decentralize production and make the whole thing more environmentally sustainable. We have the lab, we have the equipment, we have the research. We just need funding to hold onto our staff."

The commissioner from Stevens County said, "Mr. Chair, I move that we recommend to our counties that we each provide $30,000 in funding to help continue this vital work."

John said, "There's a motion on the floor. Is there a second?" A long pause followed. John looked up and down the table and finally said, "I'll second the motion, just so we can talk about this a little. Discussion?"

"Yeah." It was the commissioner from Traverse. "This is dumb. Of course, Stevens County is in favor. They're the ones who will be losing the professor job. Nothing personal, but we each kick in 30 grand and it all just goes right to Stevens County paychecks. The rest of us, no way we can support this. It isn't our problem, we won't get anything out of it, and we can't afford it."

"Hang onto that thought," John interrupted. "I'm declaring a ten-minute break. Enough time to recycle some coffee." He tapped the gavel on the table and headed for the bathroom.

The commissioner from Traverse ended up at the next urinal.

"Johnny, what the hell are you doing? That motion's dumber than shit. We can barely keep the roads plowed and the meth houses under control. We got no business trying to fund the University of Minnesota. They need to take care of themselves."

"Yeah, maybe," John said. He stared ahead, Bobby's words returning to him.

Who cares what it costs if it's the difference between lights on and lights off.

"It seems to me, maybe this is a little our business. We got five votes on the board. Stevens County will vote for it; he's got no choice. I think I'll vote for it—I got kind of a wild hair about it. And then I was thinking of you, and that County Ditch 37 that flows out of Big Stone and across your land. You've got what—eight, nine hundred acres in that watershed and you're paying the bulk of the property taxes to maintain it, even though farmers all around you are also tiling and draining. You've been wanting that thing redetermined for years, so some of the people who benefit would be paying some of the cost. I think that's a good idea, an idea whose time has maybe come." He turned and looked him square in the eye. "What do you think?"

"Jesus, Johnny, you know what I think. That damn ditch costs me a fortune. But it's going to be nothing but trouble for you. It's going to cost people a bunch of money, and almost everybody who pays is someone who votes in your district. Are you sure about this?"

"No. But I'm going to do it." He zipped up, walked to the sink, pumped out some liquid soap, and washed his hands. Looking in the mirror, he locked eyes with his colleague. "Or, at least I will if I feel the spirit of inter-county cooperation is alive and well."

On the way back to the meeting room, John saw the chancellor getting a cup of coffee. He walked up to her, poured himself a cup of coffee, and said quietly, "Chancellor, I think this could very well break your way." She looked startled, then skeptical. "There's a couple reasons. One, I think you make a good point: we should do what we can to keep science on the march. But there's another reason." He turned, leaned on the counter, and looked her in the eyes. "We live in a hard old world, Chancellor, and sometimes friends are the only thing that gets you through. If dark days should happen to come down on us, you could do worse than remember that you've got friends over in Big Stone County."

John smiled, with a smile that didn't quite reach his eyes, then he touched her shoulder and headed back to his chair. With a sinking stomach and a pounding heart, he made another check mark on his list.

THE REASON WHY

AMY WALKED DOWN THE QUIET HALL from her classroom toward the teachers' lounge, enjoying the sound of her heels bouncing off the cinder block walls. It had been a long day so far. One of her regular aides had called in sick, and bringing a substitute into the room was always disrupting. There'd already been a couple of meltdowns, including one from Suzy, an ordinarily well-behaved eight-year-old with Down's. She hadn't really seen that one coming, and her thoughts were on possible reasons when she passed the door of the gym and saw Bobby leaning against the wall by the trophy case. She paused at the foot of the stairs and looked up at him, then slowly went up the steps.

He looked good. He was wearing a long-sleeved white linen shirt, clean blue jeans, and his ever-present moccasins.

Something caught her eye. "Good Lord," she said. "Are you wearing *socks*?"

He was offended. "I'm not a barbarian, you know. I can blend in."

Amy laughed. "Bobby, the only thing you have going for you is that you never blend in, not matter where you are. So, what's up?"

"I checked in at the office, so they'd know I wasn't a terrorist, and they told me this is your prep time; you'd have a whole hour off. Could we, you know, step outside, or is that against the teacher's creed?"

Amy tilted her head and looked up at him. "Yeah, well, I guess I can take a chance."

They crossed the street to the baseball field and sat down on the bleachers.

"Glory days," Bobby said, gazing out across the pitcher's mound.

"I thought you hated baseball," Amy said.

"I do," Bobby said, "but that's because I suck at it. Besides, I think it's the law or something that you have to say, 'Glory days' when you sit down next to a ball diamond." He pulled a pair of sunglasses out of his shirt pocket and put them on.

They sat quietly for a few moments. Two blocks away, they could hear the shouts of a crew erecting a new grain bin at the grain elevator. "I'm worried about your husband," Bobby said.

"Me too," Amy said.

"He's taking this save-the-world shit way too seriously."

"He takes everything seriously, always has. Do you think he's wrong?"

"Damned if I know. Traditionally, the end of the world has been a little hard to predict."

"Come on, Bobby."

Bobby gave her an exasperated look. "Something's happening, Amy. You know that. The world is getting warmer, the weather is getting worse, the crazy people are getting crazier, the politicians are just as stupid as ever. Everything might go to hell tomorrow, or things might slide slowly downhill for the next hundred years. Or else, next week some guy with a pocket protector will come up with a nifty, swifty way to fix everything. Nobody knows, Amy, nobody has a freakin' clue. Not even your husband. Jesus, Amy, he's just a farmer. How can he think he's got a handle on the true truth?"

"So you think he's wrong?"

Bobby sighed. "I didn't say that, Amy. I said he's getting wound a little too tight."

"Who are you to talk? You're wearing socks, for Pete's sake. What's up with that?"

Bobby stretched his legs out. "Purty, ain't they. Naw, I'm going to Norway and I'm not going to walk through that security stuff barefoot. Lots of germs in airports."

Amy laughed. "That is a stunning statement. When I think of the state of your house, *now* you're worried about germs." Her voice trailed off into a giggle, and then, after a moment, she said, "So, Norway. What's in Norway?"

"I'm going look at some wind-to-hydrogen stuff, then go to Denmark and check out a thing for turning switchgrass into pellets. And then there's this city in Ireland that's trying to become totally energy independent, plus a 40-acre greenhouse in Germany that they heat with the waste heat from a power plant. They're all in the same neighborhood, so I thought I'd check them out. On the way home, I thought I'd layover in New York and spend some time in the Strand Bookstore."

"That ginormous book store in Greenwich Village?"

"Yeah. I started thinking about the amount of time I spend on the Internet looking stuff up and couldn't help but wonder what would happen if I went to log in and nothing happened. I thought I'd buy a few hundred pounds of actual books."

"And you say John is taking this stuff too seriously?"

Bobby shrugged. "I got nothing else to do, I haven't been to Europe in a while—sounded like a good excuse. Can we get back to talking about your husband?"

Amy shrugged helplessly. "Bobby, what do you want me to say? John is who he is, and he does what he's going to do. I can't even get him to wear a blue shirt with his suit. He's locked into this."

"Well, geez, I'm glad we had this talk. You've been a lot of help." Bobby stood up and stretched. "I better hit the road. My plane leaves tonight. I just have time to get to the Cities, eat at that dim sum place off 494, and catch the plane. I'll sleep all the way to Oslo.

I wish your husband was excited about getting a decent Thai restaurant here. That would really be useful." He climbed down the bleachers and then turned to look back at Amy, his sunglasses opaque against the noon sun. His voice softened, became almost inaudible.

"Amy, you know, when we were in high school, you, me, and John and, you know, I was good-looking, and smart, and funny, and you didn't know I was going to be rich, but I knew it. I just always wondered, how come you chose John?"

"Oh, Bobby," Amy said, "I don't want to do this."

"Seriously," Bobby said, "I always wondered. Don't worry, you can't hurt my feelings."

"Well, you were already a drunk. That was maybe a factor." Amy's face melted into a helpless smile, a remembrance of times past. "But, Bobby, the thing is, John gets up every morning and spends the whole day trying to be a better man, and he does that just on the off chance that I might notice. And he's so serious about it. That's kind of endearing." She ticked off another point on her fingers. "John never says anything he doesn't mean; you never mean anything you say." She paused, trying to make the next words accurate. "Bobby, when we were teenagers, you wanted to get me naked, but John wanted to be my hero. I'm sorry, Bobby, but you're still a boy, and a boy just doesn't stand a chance when he's competing with a man."

Bobby laughed. "Yeah, I was wrong." The tone of his voice made her glad she couldn't see what was behind his glasses. "Turns out you can hurt my feelings." He turned to leave but squeezed her shoulder in passing. "Well, I'm off. You want me to bring you a leprechaun, or a reindeer or something?"

"Whatever you can get through customs," Amy said, "I'll leave it up to your good judgment." She watched as Bobby crossed the street, waiting as a tractor pulling a gravity box passed by on the way to the grain elevator. He climbed into his Escalade and headed east. Amy enjoyed the sunshine for another couple minutes, then went back into the school, her mind already full of what she was going to do to help Suzy regain her composure in time for the afternoon classes.

SUCKING IN

IT WASN'T YET FIRST LIGHT when Amy made her way downstairs. A hard wind out of the east was rattling the old windows, and there was an occasional spatter of rain. John was seated in his recliner, his face lit by the pale glow of the laptop, his scarred bare feet and crooked toes looking oddly vulnerable.

"Hey," Amy said, "It's four in the morning."

John shrugged. "Couldn't really sleep, so rather than stare at the ceiling, I decided to come down and catch up on the news."

Amy sat on the arm of the chair and rubbed the back of his neck. "That might have been a mistake. You may never sleep again."

John's fingers danced across the keyboard. "Look at this, Amy, this thing in the *New York Times* from Africa. The people there are just screwed. Crappy governments, on the short edge of the global warming stick. They're just screwed, and I think they know it and they're acting like it. It's like Europe 500 years ago : warlords and fruitcake religious leaders flailing around in every direction, and all the poor, beat-up, regular folks are just ducking, trying to stay out of the way. And in Antarctica, the Wilkin Ice Shelf is melting away. Hell, I lived 40 years before I'd ever heard of the Wilkin Ice Shelf, and now I got scientists telling me this is the canary in the coal mine, we're on an escalator to hell and no stop button."

He'd started out tired and measured, but soon the words were spilling out and his voice rose in indignation.

"And in the Middle East, those scary bastards are working up their nerve to strap bombs to more retarded women and send them ambling into a market. And here, right here in the US of A, no one seems to be taking any of it seriously. This whole freakin' thing is just going down the tubes and we're spending all our time talking about gay marriage and what it costs to hire a hooker in Washington."

"In South America, our government spent a hundred years helping the fruit companies screw damn near every country south of the equator, and now they're all thinking it's time to play catch up—and those are the *good* guys to buy oil from. Even the goddamn Norwegians are going to start killing whales again, just for the hell of it. For Pete's sake, if you can't trust the goddamn Norwegians to be thoughtful and reasonable, what the hell? I mean *what the hell?*"

"And?" Amy asked.

John leaned back and rubbed his hands across his eyes. "And I'm fed up with county government. My fellow commissioners could give a shit. All they want is for no angry voters to call, so they spend their time screwing around with their expense forms, trying to sneak a beer past the auditor. And the employees think they matter. They think that everyone in the county has their eyes on the courthouse, watching in awe, and the truth is, no one cares. If the courthouse fell in the river, most people wouldn't even notice until they needed a marriage license or their roads weren't plowed."

"There's work to be done, real work, and we're not getting it done because no one seems to know what matters and what doesn't. And if I were gone tomorrow, no one would even notice; in six months they'd be talking about who the commissioners were, and they'd be snapping their fingers and going, 'And who was that guy, you know, that guy a while ago from out in Otrey.'" His last words and he was still, except for his restless fingers on the keyboard.

Amy said, "Well, I'm glad I got up and came down."

John laughed, a harsh sound with no mirth in it. "Aww shit, Amy. Go back to bed. I'm about done here. I'll go do chicken chores and start on my book-work."

Amy asked, "You sure you don't want to come back to bed?" Her soft fingers tickled the back of his neck.

John said, "Yeah, I'm sure. I got lots to do, and I know I wouldn't sleep." Amy stood up and headed for the stairs. "I wasn't talking about sleeping." There was an edge to her voice that was not at all common.

John heard the warning note and looked up, fully aware for the first time. "Hey, Amy, I'm sorry, I just..."

She kept walking but lifted one arm like a stop sign. John shut up and watched her go, listening until her footsteps faded away. When he was once again alone in the dark, he looked back into the computer and began to type. He leaned further into the blue glow of the screen as numbers and maps flowed and flickered and pulled him in.

WASTE NOT, WANT NOT

"WHAT'S NEXT?" It was nearly noon and the commissioners were getting itchy. It had been a long meeting, and stomachs were roiling with bad coffee and grocery store rolls.

"Environmental Office—the waste guys want a new contract. Ted, you have the floor."

The environmental service officer moved to the front of the room and plopped down in a chair. His belly strained against the pearl buttons of his cowboy shirt, and he wheezed a little as he arranged his papers in front of him. "Yeah," he said, pushing his glasses up on top of his bald head and smoothing his white brush of a mustache. "Ahh, here's the deal. Rural Waste says their costs for hauling our garbage have gone up. Landfills in North Dakota, gas cost, all that stuff adds up, so they're looking at a fifteen percent increase for the next five-year contract."

"What the hell?" Alan said. "Fifteen percent? How much money is that?"

"Well, we pay about three hundred grand a year, so bump that up by another forty-five. But we got no choice. Rural Waste is the only game in town—no one else hauls garbage or does recycling. They've got us over a barrel." He smirked a little, enjoying his pun.

"Well, yeah," Alan said. "Is there a motion to approve the new contract? I really want to get the hell out of here."

John sat at the end of the table. He was leaning over, his head in his hands, rubbing his hairline. "You know," he said, "Three hundred and forty-five thousand dollars is a lot of money. That would service a lot of debt. We could take that money and make a bond payment of five or six million dollars. Has anyone looked into some sort of burner here in the county, so we handle all our stuff ourselves? Shoot, it wouldn't even have to be cheaper. If it cost the same, we'd be money ahead because we're spending all that money inside the county, paying wages to our own constituents, instead of sending it off to the Mafia in New Jersey or wherever it goes."

"What do you think about that, Ted?" Alan asked.

"Well, I don't know," Ted said slowly. "Right now, we got no problems. The trucks show up and our stuff goes away." He shook his head, "What you're talking about is a lot, a lot, of bother. Are you sure you want to get involved in something like that?"

John gave a ghost of a smile. He could hear the restrained panic in Ted's voice. Right now, between morning and afternoon coffee, lunch break, and the time he spent lurking in the bathroom, Ted really was only at work about four hours a day. With a multimillion-dollar building project and all the management time that would go into running a waste-to-energy program, his easy slide into retirement could turn into a real job.

"Well, I've been thinking about this," John said, "and it seems to me that you're plenty busy as is. I just don't think it would be fair to saddle you with something like this. No, I was thinking we'd run this as a separate project, not through your office. We'd sure want to solicit your expert input though. I don't see how we could do it without your expertise. How much stuff are we talking about? Do the math." John watched carefully. Ted was a problem, like a squeaky bearing or a weedy bean field, but problems were made to be solved.

Ted shrugged, "Figure four pounds of waste per person per day. For Big Stone County, that's 20,000 pounds a day—that's 3,500 tons a year. Where you going to bury that?"

John leaned back in his chair, stretched, and wrapped his hands around the back of his head. "We're not going to bury it. We're going to sort out the recyclables and sell 'em, we're going to make compost out of the stuff that'll rot, and we'll burn the rest and make electricity with it. What do you think?"

Alan said, "John, I think you're crazy."

"Yeah, well, other than that."

Ted stammered, "Well, I don't know. I suppose there are grants and stuff. The county could bond for the building, maybe get some sort of pilot waste-to-energy program through the state." Almost against his will, Ted's mind started to race through all the possibilities that a lifetime of bureaucratic maneuvering had prepared him for.

John shook his head, "I just don't know, Ted. That just seems like too much work for one man. I mean, we're talking millions of dollars, a lot of responsibility. If you were going to ramrod this, we'd have to get your job regraded—maybe bump you up a grade and hire you some help. Of course, then the problem is that you might end up paying a fortune in income tax." A few chuckles floated around the room. "Tell you what, if it kills you from overwork, we'd name it the Ted Swanson Memorial Garbage Disposerium. Hell, we can run you through with the first batch, turn you into mulch. It'd be a hell of an honor."

John joined in the general laughter in the room. He'd seen the gleam come into Ted's eyes and knew he'd won. Right now, he laughed.

He'd throw up later.

EAT EVERYTHING

BOBBY DROVE INTO JOHN'S YARD. The old hog barns were long gone—John had torn them down, saved the lumber, and then buried the foundations. A weed-free garden flourished where they'd been. The small two-story house sat foursquare in the middle of the lawn, a tidy flower garden on the south side. A long white machine shed stretched east and west, and a gleaming silver combine sat parked next to the fuel tanks. The air was crisp, and diamonds of dew sparkled in the grass. When Bobby got out of his vehicle, he saw a pair of boots sticking out from under the header.

"What's up?" he said, walking toward the machine. "You dead, or sleeping?"

"Bearing going out on the raddle chain, I think," John said, his voice sounding hollow and distant coming from beneath the machine. "There's something making a racket down here. Would you get me a big screwdriver, please?"

"Sure. Where is it?"

"Go in the shop door. Turn left. Against the back wall, you'll see a big red toolbox. Screwdrivers should be in the second drawer from the top, on the left. Just bring the biggest one."

A few minutes later, John said, "Yeah, there it is. We got us a wobble." He slid out from underneath the combine and stood up, brushing straw and chaff off his clothes and dusting off the back of his jeans. Despite the cool of the morning, sweat darkened his T-shirt. "You want to ride with to Madison? I gotta get some parts."

"Sure," Bobby said. "I'll even drive."

John went into the house and grabbed his checkbook, then jumped into the front seat of the Escalade, pushing a litter of fast-food wrappers to one side. "What's it cost to fill this thing with gas?"

Bobby shrugged, "If you have to ask, you can't afford it. It's got to cost a hell of a lot less than running your equipment."

"Couple grand a day, just to keep the wheels turning, and that's if I don't need to put fuel in the semi. Is it going to end?"

"Who knows? I don't, that's for sure."

The miles passed in mild conversation, and a half hour later they pulled up in front of the implement dealership. John and Bobby got out, walked past several million dollars' worth of tractors and combines and a $12,000 lawnmower, then into the dimly lit building. Oil filters, sickle sections, and chainsaw displays lined the walls, and their footsteps echoed off the cement floor. The air was cool and scented faintly with parts cleaner and hydraulic oil. The parts counter was thirty feet long, covered with greasy plastic, and dotted with computer terminals.

The parts man was perched on a tall stool, hunched over a keyboard.

"Hey John," he said, looking up, "what can I do you for?"

"Lower feeder house bearing, R62."

The parts man didn't look up but asked, "Do you want them both? Might as well, I'd recommend it."

"Yeah, okay."

After a few seconds, a printer whirred and spit out a receipt. The parts man glanced at it for a location number, then disappeared into the labyrinth of shelves. He appeared shortly, carrying two greasy packages, which he thumped down on the counter. John glanced at the receipt, made a face, and wrote out a check. He mumbled thanks and headed toward the door.

"Hey John," the parts man said, "do you know why they bury lawyers twenty-six feet deep?"

John paused. "No, I don't know why they bury lawyers twenty-six feet deep. Why?"

"Cause deep down, they're nice guys."

John looked back, tilted his head, and smiled. He waved a hand and continued toward the door.

Once back in the car and headed north, Bobby said, "Have you ever heard of Tikopia?"

"We had some at the Matador once. I thought it tasted like crap."

"No, you clown, not tilapia. Tikopia. It's an island in the South Pacific. Dude named Jared Diamond wrote a book called *Collapse* and he talked about it."

"Bobby, you know more shit that don't matter than anyone I know."

"No, no, no, this does matter. This island is about the size of your farm, about two square miles, and it's out in the middle of nowhere and it's kept a thousand people or so alive for thousands of years."

"Well, yeah, it's in the South Pacific. You just lay around and catch coconuts. How hard can it be?"

"I think maybe it's a little harder than that. But that's the deal. They got trees, trees lining all the fields, and all the trees have some sort of edible fruit or something. They don't always use it, but when times are tough, there's this food ready to hand. How many trees do we plant in Big Stone County?"

"I dunno. The soil conservation district must plant thousands every year."

"Yeah, and there it is. They pretty much plant ash and poplar, things like that. But they don't need to. They could plant black walnut, hickory, butternut, hazelnut. Stuff like that. They'd stop the wind just as well, provide just as much shade, be just as good at erosion control, so if they'll still do what they're supposed to do, why not get a little extra benefit? I mean, what the hell?"

"What the hell indeed. Well, the soil conservation district is coming in to talk budget. I can maybe have a chat. You going to help me change these bearings?"

IT TAKES A VILLAGE

AMY LOOKED UP FROM THE NEWSPAPER. "Hey darlin'," she said, "did you see this article about the new survivalists? People think a big crash is coming and they're planting gardens and trees and such."

"Freakin' morons," John grunted.

"Excuse me?" Amy said. "What exactly have you been doing? How are they the morons?"

John shrugged. "Can't work. One family on their own. Margins are too tight, no economy of scale. Look," he went on, "say you butcher a hog. You get a hundred pounds of meat, but you're living out in the woods with no electricity. What the hell you going to do with that much meat? Can't freeze it—no electricity. Maybe you could can it, but that's tricky; there's going to be a hell of a lot of survivalists dead of botulism. How many people do you know who still can their own food? And you're not going to have just one hog—you'll have a whole litter, maybe eight or ten butcher hogs all ready at the same time, so that's a thousand pounds of meat you need to deal with—and that's the best-case scenario. Worst case is your sow doesn't get bred and you got no pigs at all."

"Now, say you're a community. You butcher a hog and four hundred people each have a little pork for dinner—no fuss, no waste. And tomorrow you have beef, or chicken. You've got enough people so some can specialize in different crafts, like blacksmith or doctor—jobs that you don't get good at if you do them part time. You get four, five hundred people working together, you've got something. You try and do it yourself, you're just a nut in the woods looking over your shoulder for some other nut and watching your kids die of appendicitis."

Amy looked at him. "You're a cheery guy, John. Have I ever told you that?"

John laughed deep in his throat. "Yeah, call me Mr. Sunshine. I've been thinking about this a lot, and Bobby, he's done nothing but think about this. You want to hear his lecture on Dunbar's Number? There's a reason people have been gathering in villages for the last ten thousand years."

"How come no one else talks like this?"

"Cause the people who write books are city people, and city people are stupid."

"C'mon, John, you don't believe that."

"Oh hell yes. People who live in a city live with the expectation that someone will take care of them. If they get a flat tire, they call Triple A. If someone busts a window on their house, they call the cops, and they expect the grocery stores to always have food for them. Actually, a lot of city people hardly cook. How many of them realize that if the trucks stop running, they're hungry in a couple days and starving in a week and they don't have the slightest freakin' clue what to do about it. Remember 9/11? All those people dying in those big damn buildings. Thousands of people worked in those buildings and you know, when the fire got bad, I kept expecting someone to bust out a window and jump out with a parachute they kept under their desk, but no one did."

"John," Amy protested, "nobody expected anyone in the Towers to strap on a parachute they kept under their desk."

"I did. I did." The words came out slowly, with a hard emphasis. "I kept waiting for a parachute or a hang glider or some damn thing. Not one person! Why would you spend every day of your life going to a place to work where you were completely dependent on other people to keep you alive? What were they thinking? No one took five minutes to think about how to take care of themselves, but instead just left their lives all up to the experts, and the experts screwed up."

Amy stared at him, open-mouthed, seeing something she'd never seen before. She started to say something, then settled back in her chair, listening.

John got up from the table and roamed around the dining room, straightening pictures and rubbing the dust off the top of the buffet. "'Cause that's what experts do," he said. "They screw up. They think they know everything and they don't know shit, and they don't know what they don't know. And when everything falls apart, they say 'Oops' and go find a consulting job teaching the lessons of the disaster they didn't see coming."

He looked at the palms of his hands and rubbed them together, a tiny whispery sound coming up into the air. "They don't know shit, Amy. And they don't care about us."

He looked at his hands again, then lifted his eyes and met Amy's across the table. "Amy, they don't care."

ALMOST READY

"I THINK I'M DONE," John said. "Windmills are up, biomass plant is up, research at the U is ongoing, tree program is up, pretty much all the shit we talked about is either done or undoable. And, of course, every voter in the county thinks I'm a freakin' moron."

"You going to run for re-election?" Bobby asked.

"Yeah, I think so."

"You know," Bobby said, "you're going to get your ass kicked. Everybody is pissed at you. Already, five people have filed. You might not even make it out of the primary."

John shrugged. "I can't not try, Bobby. I can't just not file and slink off into the sunset. Besides, did you see who's running? Those guys could fuck up a two-car funeral."

"Doesn't matter," Bobby said, "you know that. People's taxes are up and strange things are going on. People live here because they want things not to change. You're running around telling folks things they don't want to hear and you're spending their money like water. I'm telling you, John, you're going to get your ass kicked."

"And I'm telling you, I can't just not try. I can't."

"So what do you want to do?"

"Oh, Christ, I never do what I want to do." He looked at the ceiling and then turned to look Bobby in the eye. "What I want to do is move to Norway. Way up north, where it's dark all the time. I want to live in a little cabin and spend my time eating unpalatable food—too much of it—and stare into a sputtering fire until my body melds with the tattered sheets." He held Bobby's gaze and then shrugged and turned away.

Bobby took a deep breath, looked down at his hands, and noticed a slight tremble. He stared at John's rigid back and then said into a vast silence, "Okay, if that's what you want to do, what are you going to do?"

John shrugged again. "File for re-election, get ready to get my ass kicked. Besides, it doesn't matter anymore. I've done what I can do. If nothing bad happens, if the world just keeps plodding along, I haven't caused any real harm. And if the end of the world does come sailing in, I've done all I can to get ready."

Bobby said, "Do you really believe that?"

John met his eyes, stared steadily at him. "I don't really believe much, Bobby." He continued to stare for a few more seconds and then turned to look out the windows, across the fields. "I believe I'm tired. I believe I'm sick of people and sick of the stupid, selfish things they do. Everything that's wrong around us, all of it, is no big deal—nothing that couldn't be fixed if people would just get their heads out of their asses. I'm just so sad at it all. It's all so wrong and it doesn't need to be. I used to be mad, but now I'm just sad." He took a deep breath but didn't turn around.

"Besides, Bobby, I've done what I can. What happens from here on out don't mean shit."

END OF THE BEGINNING

IT WAS THE BEGINNING OF AUGUST. The lawns were dry and the fields lush. The morning sun was hot and the air already sticky.

"John," Amy said, "something's eating the sweet corn."

"Yeah, I saw that," John said. "I think it was coons. Don't worry, I've got a plan. I think there's a den out along the slough. I'll go out there, shove a shotgun in the hole, and roust 'em out."

"Okay," Amy said doubtfully. "Be careful. I'm going in to school to work on my room a little. I'll probably have lunch with Ruth."

John flipped a hand and jumped on the four-wheeler to check for weeds in a late-planted field of beans. There were some: a few thistles and some lambsquarters. He turned off the engine and leaned back in the seat while he dialed the co-op on his cell phone. The engine cracked and popped as it cooled, and the warmth rose along the inside of his legs. "Hey, Lee," he said, "could you spray my beans in Section 6?" He listened for a moment, then said, "Yeah, whenever, doesn't matter. The thistles are a couple weeks away from blossoming."

The engine started at a touch of a button. He'd just put in new plugs and cleaned the gas tank of a couple years' accumulated crud. Back at the house, he checked the salt in the water softener and retrieved a shotgun from the gun rack. Looking through the boxes of ammunition, he settled on number two buckshot. With 15 pellets, each about the size of a .22 slug, it should do the job.

He stood in the middle of the yard and looked around. He'd finished painting the house, the lawn was mowed, and the garage doors worked. He'd paid all the bills and checked to make sure all the insurance was up to date. When he examined his world, it all looked done.

He walked out along the edge of the slough, where the bank dropped off steeply toward the cattails, toward a spot he'd noticed a week ago. An old box elder tree perched right on the top of the slope, had a branch about the size of the tip of his finger broken off a few inches from the trunk. The sun beat down, sweat dripping into the small of his back. The cloth of his shirt was hot on his shoulders. He stood on the very brink of the slope and looked around thoughtfully. A scuff mark on the edge and it would all make sense to whoever found him. Sweating, he carefully eased the shotgun's trigger guard over the branch and socketed the muzzle tight against his armpit. This would work. The gun would go off and he'd slip over the edge and land in a heap at the bottom. The number two buckshot should shred his heart and turn his lights off almost instantly. Even if that didn't happen, no one would be looking for him for half a day or more, and there was no doubt in his mind that no one would find him alive. When they did find him, they'd guess that he'd slipped, dropped the shotgun, and just, through massive bad luck, had the trigger catch on a tree branch. It wouldn't look like suicide and it wouldn't look like he'd been stupid. Both were very important to him.

He took a final look around the horizon he'd seen every day of his life and then looked down to get his feet placed properly.

He paused. This shouldn't just end.

"I'm sorry, Amy," he said out loud, "but you can take care of yourself and I'm just so tired."

He took a deep breath, his pulse pounding in his ears, and then became aware of a distant shout.

"John," he heard, "John, where are you? I need you." There was a note of joy in her voice he'd never heard before. He looked yearningly down the slope and carefully moved the shotgun away from his body. He paused while a drop of sweat slid off the tip of his thumb. He reached down and snicked the safety on.

He was dripping sweat by the time he got back to the farmyard. Amy saw him and came running across the lawn. "Sarah called, Sarah called, Sarah called," she caroled. "Buddy, you're gonna be a grandpa."

"Really," he said. "Well, I'll be go to hell."

She planted a kiss on his lips and spun away back toward the house. "She's three months along," she shouted over her shoulder. "She didn't want to call until the doctor told her the coast was clear. I've got about thirty calls to make."

She disappeared into the house, and John slowly followed her. He stopped at the gun rack, emptied the shotgun, and put it back on the rack. He closed the box of shells and put them on the top shelf. "Well, shit," he said.

"What'd you say?" Amy asked from the other room.

"Nothing," John said. "I just said, 'Better get back to work.'" He looked in the mirror on the way out. Hollow, red-rimmed eyes looked back at him, and the sweat drying on his back made him shiver. "Back to work."

JANUARY COLD

IT WAS A JANUARY COLD in western Minnesota. The snow was hard and squeaked underfoot. Bobby took a deep breath as he climbed out of his car and savored the pain as it swirled down into his lungs. The sun was an orange semicircle on the eastern horizon, with the bright shadows of two sun dogs already evident on each side. He glanced toward the house, saw that the lights were off, and headed toward the shop, which, despite the early hour, already had a plume of black smoke coming out the chimney. He opened the side door and left the world of bright cold behind. The shop was dimly lit, with smoke in the air and an AM radio sputtering on a shelf. Cold by the door, the room temperature went up dramatically the closer he got to the stove. A hard blue light flickering on the walls warned him, and he shielded his eyes as he rounded the edge of the stove.

John was hunched over a welding table, looking like a troll in a black welding helmet and filthy coveralls. With steady delicacy, the TIG nozzle and filler wire danced across two pieces of aluminum. Bobby stood and watched through slitted eyes until John reached the end of the weld and took his foot off the voltage control. The bright light died, and he stood up straight and stretched.

"I didn't know you knew how to weld aluminum," Bobby said.

"Shit, I can do anything," John said, raising his helmet, "except sing and dance."

Bobby moved closer and ran his finger over the weld. "Nice. What're you making?"

"The key," John said, rolling his shoulders and taking his welding helmet off, "is to wipe the metal with alcohol before you start. Gotta get rid of the impurities or you get voids in the weld." He stomped his feet and yawned widely. "I'm making a greenhouse. Had some aluminum channel left over from when I tore down the hoghouse and it seemed like just the ticket."

"What do you know about greenhouses?"

"Damn little. But I know how to grow stuff and how to make stuff. That should get me started."

"Okay... you got time to make me a cup of coffee?"

"I don't even have a job. I got all the time in the world." He reached out with the toe of his work boot and flipped off the power switch on the welder, then led the way out of the shop. Once outside, Bobby glanced up at the chimney, still belching black smoke, and asked, "What the hell are you burning in that thing?"

John looked and said, "I got an old sprayer nozzle hooked up to a five-gallon can of used oil. When the fire gets hot enough, the oil thins out and runs through the nozzle into the firebox."

"Is that environmentally sound?"

"I'd have to say no. I don't even think it's legal. Luckily, now that I'm no longer a county commissioner, I don't have to worry about setting a good example. Next year I'm thinking of voting Republican and cooking meth."

"Heading for complete depravity, are we?"

"Yeah, pretty much." He kicked off his boots in the entryway of the house, then struggled out of his winter coat and coveralls, leaving them in a pile. Bobby took off his sneakers and zipped down his coat before following him into the kitchen.

It was warm and smelled of coffee and cinnamon. Two coffee cups and a cereal bowl were in the sink, and a crockpot sat on the counter. Bobby peered in and saw a beef roast with a can of mushroom soup dumped on top of it. "Is that lunch?" he asked.

"Not for you," John said. "I'm hoping it will be ready for supper." He checked the phone for messages and then sat at the kitchen table. "Got some cookies, though. Amy was up at five baking for the funeral. She didn't take them all with her, which makes them fair game as far as I'm concerned. Grab the coffee, will ya?" He made a tidy pile out of a scattering of books and magazines on the table. "Don't tell Amy I let you in here when the place was such a dump."

"No problem. Who died?"

"You know—Elmer what's'isname... Wood. That old guy who lived by himself west of town. Turns out he was baptized in our church, hasn't been back since, but that makes putting him in the ground our problem."

Bobby laughed. "John, you are one hell of a Christian. I'm a little inspired just to hear the depth of your concern for Mr. Wood's immortal soul."

John smiled. "Poor old bastard. I don't think he even had running water, except in the barn. He's got no family. The bank asked me to go over there and look things over. He's got about twenty draft horses—huge things—enough hay for twenty years, and nothing else. Shit, he was dead a week before the mailman got curious and called the sheriff."

"What happened to him?"

"Who knows? He was an old guy who lived on cigarettes and canned soup. He just died."

"What are they going to do with the horses?"

"There's a big 'who knows' too. They're mixed breeds, nothing purebred, nothing anyone else would want to buy except maybe the Amish. I think he just kept them for pets. Nobody slaughters horses anymore—I don't even think it's legal. I don't know what you do with horses that nobody wants. I'll just go over there every few days and roll a big bale of hay into the pasture and make sure the water tank's full. The bank can sort the rest out."

"Maybe you should bring them over here."

"Yeah, maybe not. What the hell would I do with a bunch of horses?"

"You could get completely off the grid then."

"Could. But how would I feed the horses when all my money would be going to alimony payments? Amy still dreams of flying first class some day. I can't really see her as a pioneer woman." He reached for another cookie and leaned back in his chair. It was old and wooden, with a broken rung in the front and the right side of the seat scarred and dented from thirty years of contact with his pliers holster. "I'm only allowed to sit in one chair—how much influence do you really think I have?"

Bobby poured another cup of coffee, then went to the refrigerator, rummaged around, and found a pint of whipping cream. He dumped in a healthy dollop and came and sat down again. "So what else is new?"

"Damnedest thing," John said. "Right before the first of the year, I decided to buy a bunch of seed and stuff ahead of time."

"You know," Bobby said, "farming ought to be against the law. Do you just decide how much income tax you want to pay?"

"Yeah, pretty much. Anyway, I wanted to buy some corn seed and take delivery, so the IRS wouldn't get testy. And Bert said I couldn't do it—I could pay for the corn and it'd be on the books, but I couldn't take delivery. Turns out about two-thirds of the corn seed is grown in South America during the winter—it won't even get here until a month before planting. Who'd have thunk it?"

Bobby shrugged. "Just-in-time manufacturing. That's nothing new. Everyone's doing it."

"Yeah, okay, but if a shipment of car parts is late, I have to wait a week for my new Chevy. If the corn seed isn't here on time, I don't know what happens. Nothing good, that's for sure."

Bobby chuckled, but the line between his eyes deepened. "What are you going to do about it?"

John said, "What the hell do you think? Bitch and put up with it. Do you think Monsanto or Pioneer Seeds gives a shit what I think?" He took a last drink of coffee and then asked, "What can I do for you, anyway? Out of coffee, or just looking to waste my time?"

"You don't even have a job—you've got nothing but time to waste. No, I just stopped in to see how things are going."

John looked around the kitchen and then met Bobby's eye. "I'm going to be a grandpa pretty soon. Everything else sorta pales in comparison to that. Amy is going out of her gourd."

"How's Sarah doing?"

John shook his head sideways, more of a twitch than anything else. "I don't know. I get the feeling like this baby thing wasn't really in the plans. The last few times we've called, Stan is never around. She hasn't said anything, but I just get the feeling that all is not quite as it should be."

"Hey, some guys get nuts thinking about a baby. Tied down for the next twenty years, wife with stretch marks, all that stuff."

John laughed out loud. His chair legs thumped down and he choked on a bite of cookie. After a short bout of coughing, he finally managed to say, "Jesus Christ, Bobby. You know less about marriage than my dog. What the hell? Have you been reading *Cosmo* again?"

Bobby said defensively, "I was just trying to make you feel better. Well, fuck you."

John was still chuckling. "No, man, it's okay. I'm not laughing at you. No, no, I guess I am laughing at you. No, really, thanks for the effort." He shoved the plate across the table. "Have another cookie. But then I need to get back to work. What did you do for a New Year's adventure?"

"I stayed home, just like usual."

"I don't get that—a big-time partier, a man about town, sitting home watching Dick Clark."

Bobby shrugged. "He's dead, isn't he? New Year's is for the amateur drinkers. Besides, what if I was on the road at one in the morning and had a head-on with some drunk? I'd hate to think I'd gotten killed by some dummy full of $7-a-bottle pink champagne."

John toasted him with his coffee cup. "It's good to meet a man with standards."

On their way out the door, Bobby waited as John shrugged back into his heavy winter clothing.

"What are you going to do about your seed corn?" he asked.

"Just what I said. Bitch and try not to think about it."

IT'S BURNING

"OH MY GOD! Honey, look at that," Amy said. She was walking through the living room carrying an armful of laundry and paused in the middle of the room.

"Huh?" John asked, looking up from the magazine.

"Look, on TV."

From his perch in the recliner, John peered between his toes and saw images of towering flames coming from huge buildings and ant-sized firefighters working cautiously around the perimeter of the fires. He looked down through his bifocals and found the mute button on the remote and flipped it off.

"…dockworkers strike in the Brazilian Port of Santos turned violent today when, apparently, a cooking fire by striking workers ignited dust in a huge grain terminal. The resulting explosion left 23 people dead and the facilities badly damaged. Representatives of the port authority said…"

John hit the mute button again and shook his head. "What a hell of a mess. Bad enough when terrorists blow shit up, but look at that—some poor bastard out on strike tries to fry a hot dog and blows himself and the place he worked all to hell and gone."

Amy lifted an eyebrow. "Do they have hot dogs in Brazil?"

"I don't know," John laughed. "They have to eat something. Maybe they were frying bananas or boiling beans. I don't really think that changes my point."

"Yeah, I suppose you're right." Amy shook her head, took one last look at the TV screen, shuddered, and headed upstairs with the laundry. John went back to reading. He absentmindedly clenched and released his toes inside the heavy work boots, bending the arch away from the thick leather soles as he read. His feet hurt from a long day spent standing on cold concrete as he started the process of getting all his farm machinery refurbished before the cropping season. Truthfully, he barely noticed the pain—there had been very few days in the past quarter century when some part of his body hadn't hurt. The pain had put a furrow between his eyes, but he didn't notice the lines in his face, and he noticed the pain the way a fish noticed water.

When Amy came back downstairs, he was asleep, snoring slightly, the magazine spilled out of his relaxed hands. Every now and then, one of his legs jumped.

Amy carefully plucked the remote from his lap and made a quick pass through the TV channels. CNN had long since switched from their story on the Brazilian port to traffic problems in California and a low-grade political scandal in Vermont. She turned off the TV and the lights, then glanced back at John sleeping in the darkened room and went up to bed herself. He'd probably get cold and wake up in a couple of hours, then come to bed, where his body would be a long, cold distraction from her own sleep.

In Santos, the fires spread and burned long into the night. At 3:00 in the morning, the fires reached an ethanol loading facility and added a hot red flame, which spread across the water to other docks. Firefighters using water added to the problem, as the alcohol spread far and wide, floating on the runoff. When they started using ATC foam, they spread a blanket almost four feet thick, but the fire continued to burn. In the confusion, the police more or less accidentally shot three striking workers. It took four days to bring it completely under control, and by that time, the port was a wreck and the strike had spread across the country.

GUYS IN TIES

"BERT," JOHN SAID PATIENTLY, "It's time to plant corn. I got the land, I got the fertilizer. The equipment is hooked up and waiting at the end of the field, the sun is shining, the birds are singing. All I need, Bert, is a little seed corn."

It was the second week in April. The morning sun had enough strength to it that the two men were standing in the shadows inside John's machine shed. A couple nail holes in the roof let in tiny shafts of sunlight made visible by drifting dust motes.

"Jesus, John, I know." Bert took a deep drag on his Merit and looked without favor at the soggy butt. He shook another cigarette out of the pack and lit it from the coal of the first. He had a stringy red mustache and long arms with prominent veins and ropy muscles. A small hard paunch bulged the lower third of his snap-buttoned shirt. He squatted on his haunches, the new cigarette hanging from one corner of his mouth while he concentrated on field-stripping the remains of the first. When he finished, he stood up, ground the butt into the dust, took another deep drag, and then looked John in the eye.

"John," he said, "you're not going to get your seed corn, but you didn't hear that from me. The company is still saying any day now, but I got a phone call from a buddy at headquarters and he says, 'Bullshit.' There was a bad fire at a big port in Brazil, and now there are strikes all over South America and the seed didn't get on the boats to come up here."

"Bert, that's nuts. There's planes, there's trains, there's trucks. Hell, I don't believe there is no way to get that seed up to me."

Bert shook his head. "No, John, listen. Here's the deal. You got two seed companies that sell about 90% of the corn seed in North America. They raise about 75% of their seed in South America. Now, if they put that seed on a plane, it will cost a freakin' fortune compared to a boat. They go to all that bother and they can't charge you more—you already paid for the seed. Shit, they could have a 747 drop it right in your planter and all you'll say is, 'What kept you?' They figure, they already got your money—you and I know most guys buy their seed ahead of time. My buddy says they're going to offer to roll your dollars over into bean seed, collect insurance on lost sales, use any loss to write off against profits, and put this year's seed in the warehouse and then hang onto it until next year. They might even make more money this way, and they can blame it all on South American unions."

"But the country needs the corn."

"John," Bert said, *that's not their problem.* Jesus, John, get a clue. Their problem is profits and shareholders, and this works out for both of them. It's the guys in ties, buddy, the guys in ties."

John leaned against back and thumped his head gently against the rough timber of the machine shop frame. He ran his hands over his chin and across his eyes. "Bert," he said, "remember three years ago when bean acres went up 5% and the price dropped two bucks a bushel? What happens if bean acres go up 50%, and corn drops the same? Corn flakes will cost a hundred bucks a box and I'll have to pay someone to haul my soybeans away. It'll be a freakin' disaster."

"For you, maybe, and for me, and for a couple hundred million other poor sons a bitches, but that don't mean it won't happen." Bert took another deep drag, a third of the cigarette turning to ash. He held it between his thumb and forefinger and said, "I wish I could afford real cigarettes. Remember when I smoked Marlboros?"

"I can remember when you didn't smoke at all."

"Yeah, well, times change. I don't have nursing home insurance—I need to die young." He stepped out of the shadows and faced into the sun, squinting. "John, here's a thought for you. What if instead of *all* soybeans you plant some edible beans? Two or three kinds, that way you'll spread the risk a little. Shit, maybe even flax, wheat, and some oats. Most guys wouldn't do that—couldn't do that. What with Roundup and all the other genetic modifications, even the bad farmers can look like good farmers. You're old school enough to do it the way we used to."

"Is that a compliment?"

"Geez, John, it just is. I don't know what to say—I've known you since we were six. I'm sorry as hell I can't get you your corn. I'm just trying to give you good advice."

"Yeah, yeah, I understand." John paused and looked around. A half mile to the east, a coyote skittered across an open field in search of dinner. A quarter mile from the coyote's questing noise, a quartet of pheasants popped into the air and then disappeared into the tall grass and willows along the creek. "Okay, let's go in the house, try and figure something out. But this, this will be a long year."

They walked across the yard as a soft breeze from the south rustled through the trees, and off in the far distance, the quiet clamor of migrating geese added to the springtime symphony.

"Hey, I hear you're a grandpa," Bert said. "How's that going?"

"Ahh, it's good," John said. "Amy's having a great time. She's been going over there every weekend. I think they're coming here this weekend."

"It's a little girl, right? Three generations of women, a totally chick household. How you going to handle that?"

John shrugged. "Keep my head down, keep out of the way. You want to put that cigarette out? Amy will slit your throat if you smoke in the house the day before the baby comes to visit. Or is that part of your 'no nursing home insurance' plan?"

"Sadly enough, I can think of worse ways to go. So, what are you and the womenfolk going to do this weekend? Sit around and watch *50 First Dates*, maybe get a pedicure?"

"Yeah, I don't know. I would be getting ready to plant corn if some asshole of a seed salesman would have made a little trip to South America. That's what I would have called customer service."

"Hey, John, if I ever sneak anything back from South America, it probably isn't going to be corn seed." Bert took a last deep drag and dropped the butt to the sidewalk. "But I will tell you, John, I know three things. The world is going bat-shit crazy, it's going to get worse before it gets better, and the whole thing is the fault of the guys in ties."

John held the porch door open for him and then, with a deft sideways kick, scuffed the butt into the shrubs. He took a deep breath of springtime and smiled with no discernible mirth. "Guys in ties, buddy. Guys in ties."

Then he went into the house.

OUT THE DOOR

THE TRAFFIC ON SNELLING AVENUE was sparse. With gas at $10 a gallon, people only drove when they needed to, and with plants and businesses shutting down, fewer people had anywhere to go. Beth Hendrickson had left work early, leaving the St. Paul campus of the University of Minnesota and winding her way through the State Fair Grounds and then turning south. Her mind was racing, replaying the afternoon's conversation.

"Beth," the dean had said, "you saw the governor's budget. There's no money in the state and everybody—*everybody*—is getting slashed. We like your project, like the way you conduct research, like everything about you. It's just that you're sitting on the back of the sled and the wolves are getting closer."

"But Don," she'd said, "what I'm doing is important! We can't just quit."

"Beth. This is a land-grant university, one of the premier research facilities in the nation. Everything we do is important. It's just that not everything is going to get funded. And, you should know, it's not just you getting whacked—it's not just the bottom rung of the ladder, it's the bottom half. Everyone who hasn't been here fifteen years is gone. We'll try and find something for you, but it's not going to be much and I can't guarantee anything. I'd suggest you polish up your résumé and start looking."

"Looking where, Don?" It was the first flash of impatience she'd let show through, like a random glimpse of lightning in a stormy sky. With her height and swimmer's shoulders, she knew she could be intimidating, so over the years she'd learned to keep her blonde hair short and curly and her tone mild. But every now and then, a glimpse of blue fire sneaked out of her eyes and left people who thought they knew her unsettled. "Do you see a lot of other colleges hiring right now? I'll be lucky to get a job stacking trays in a greenhouse at a junior college."

"What the HELL do you expect me to do!" Beth rocked back in her chair, just a bit. Don had never raised his voice; she didn't think he was capable of it. He stood up and looked out the window while raking one hand through his long white hair.

"I don't know what to do," he said, his back to her and his voice soft now, and questioning. "Beth, I've had this same conversation nine times today. People I've known for years, projects I believe in and research that needs to be done, and it's all gone, and you know why? I found out why this morning—it's all going away because it doesn't fit the new paradigm. Jesus, Beth, I've been in academia for thirty years. I should be used to bullshit, but these new guys, they set a standard like none I've ever seen before."

He roughly combed his hair back into place with splayed fingers and then turned around and looked her squarely in the eye. "Go home, Beth. You don't work here anymore."

His eyes widened, as if shocked by his own candor. "There's no need to come back, because the truth is I'm not going to be able to give you anything but a terrific reference and that won't do you much good. If you hadn't taken so much time off, maybe things could have been different."

"I wasn't on vacation, Don."

Her voice was mild again, but he flinched.

"Talk to your husband and then take him and your kids someplace safe, because this is bad and it may get worse. Take whatever you want from your office—no one's going to miss it, because there won't be anyone moving in." His eyes wavered and in a flash of insight, Beth saw that he no longer looked experienced and authoritative. He just looked old. "In a reasonable world, an old crock like me would be shoved on an ice floe and this place would be filling up with young guns like you, full of piss and vinegar, ideals and good ideas. But that just isn't the way the world works, and I'm the beneficiary. I'll be drawing a paycheck until all the lights go off." He gave her a crooked smile, a mere twitch of the lips, and said, "There. That's the first time I've told the truth all day long. It doesn't feel too bad."

He sat back down at his desk, and he didn't offer to shake her hand.

She went back to her office and sat down behind her own desk. She closed her eyes, took a couple of deep breaths, and then started to work. In ten minutes, she had a half dozen thumb drives full of all the data she thought might be useful. She headed out the door with her laptop, the thumb drives, and a cardboard box full of pictures, her diplomas, and a few mementos. She stopped at the lab and used her access pass to get into the quarantine section.

Beth grabbed a parka off the wall and let herself into the giant cooler. She couldn't suppress a guilty glance over her shoulder. She had every right to be in this room, just no right to do what she was about to do. Her breath frosted the air as she paused in front of the shelves of seed samples and began scooping them into a backpack.

She did the math as she worked. Five-ounce samples of each variety of edible beans should give her twenty pounds or more after one generation, a ton or more after two. One year's crop would feed a family, two would feed a town. One hundred varieties from all over the world. Some were wrong for this climate, but some weren't, and the samples covered the whole gamut of growing conditions and regions: possible yields, disease resistance, and nutritional value.

"Talk about value-added agriculture," she muttered under her breath. "Maybe I can't get any money out of an ATM, but if I can find someone smart, I have something to trade." She shuddered briefly and closed her eyes, a dark vision passing in front of her. "Smart and honest. Smart and honest."

"HEY!"

She jumped and turned around.

The campus security guard was staring at her. She'd seen him a hundred times and had never bothered to learn his name, something she suddenly regretted. "What the hell do you think you're doing?"

"I'm just taking a few samples, for research."

"Show me your authorization," he said. "Nothing is supposed to leave this place without paperwork. You should know that."

"I am a professor," Beth said. "I've worked here for years. I have a PhD."

"I've worked here for years, too. I don't have a PhD, but I have a Taser. Guess which one means more today?"

The backpack weighed over thirty pounds. She dropped it on the floor of the cooler and set the box of diplomas and mementos next to it. Five minutes later, she was in her car. She was passing Hamline University before she started to cry. By the time she reached University Avenue, her tears were gone.

She turned right on Grand Avenue, and a few minutes later, pulled into her driveway. The house was dark, but that was to be expected. The boys were at the daycare down the street, and Abigail was still at school.

She looked around her neighborhood. She and Steve had moved here when she was pregnant with Abby. They'd taken long walks ending up at Izzy's for ice cream, attended concerts and lectures at Macalester, gotten to know the funky ins and outs of the neighborhood, made it feel like a home. An only child of only children, Beth had never really felt settled and at home anywhere, so she'd leaned into this neighborhood the way you'd lean into a campfire on a cold day.

And now it didn't feel that way anymore, and Beth felt the absence in her bones.

The house was cold. Heating expenses were through the roof, and she'd gotten in the habit of leaving the thermostat at 50 and living in sweaters and boots. They all slept in the basement in one room since Steve had left. Although the kids struggled with runny noses and coughs, their budget was stretching just far enough to keep the lights on.

She started to pack. First the double stroller for the boys—she didn't know if they'd have to walk, but she knew she couldn't carry both of them very far. All the food in the cupboards, the camping gear from the garage, and then whatever warm clothes she could stuff in the nooks and crannies.

She hesitated for a moment, then went to their upstairs bedroom and got a small locked box from the top shelf of their closet. She had to search for a moment to find the key in the nightstand, then sat down on the bed and opened the box. Inside, the pistol squatted, compact and evil-looking. She didn't even know what kind it was— Steve had showed her how to use it. "Just pull the hammer back and then pull the trigger," he'd said, "Look at what you're shooting at and keep pulling the trigger until it stops making noise." He'd made it seem like a joke, but he'd also made her practice, and the day he'd left for the job in Bismarck, he'd waited until she'd proved she could find the key before he'd kissed her goodbye. She locked the box again, walked out the door without looking back, and stored the box under the driver's seat. The key went in her pocket.

She stood in the driveway next to her car and dialed Steve's cellphone. Her heart lifted when she heard it ringing, but then sank to its more familiar depth when she heard the usual message: "The customer you have dialed is not available. Please stay on the line and leave a message at the beep." She hung up before the beep, not wishing to leave her twenty-third message.

She picked up the boys from daycare and got them safely buckled into their car seats. Daniel squirming and fighting, Sam yawning and almost asleep from a hard day playing. Abby was waiting just

inside the door of the school and came scampering down the sidewalk when she saw the car, swinging her book bag like a lariat.
"Hey, Mom," she said, jumping into the front seat and fastening her
seat belt. Beth took a moment and looked at her daughter and then
in the mirror at her two sons. Her eyes skittered off the space between the two boys.

"My three beautiful children," she said, but what she thought
was, *There used to be four, but that was before.* Her stomach turned
over at the grim rhyme and her heart teetered on the edge of a chasm.

Abby rescued her. "Guess what?" She launched into a complicated tale of homeroom squabbles and new lunchroom buddies.
Beth let her talk, basking in the warmth of her words. They were on
394 headed west before she paused, looked around, and said, "Mom,
where are we going?"

Beth looked at her oldest child and said, "Honey, we're going
to the farm."

TO THE PRAIRIE

SHE STOPPED AT A GAS STATION IN WILLMAR. The pump wouldn't take her credit card, so she went inside the brightly lit store to pay with the last of her cash.

The shelves were only half stocked, although there was a plentiful selection of locally made beef jerky.

"Hey," Beth said, keeping an eye out the window at her car in case the kids woke up. "I need $50 worth of gas."

"Sure," the young woman behind the counter said, "I'll need to see your farm-exempt permit."

"I'm sorry, I don't know what you mean?"

"Oh, traveling through? Yeah, we're only allowed to sell gas to farmers who are using it for business purposes. Sorry."

Beth felt the bottom fall out. The world around her wavered and then came sharply back into focus. The gas gauge was under a quarter and she had ninety miles yet to travel. She leaned across the counter, looked the clerk in the eye, and said, "I just need maybe three gallons. I'll give you all the money I have." She looked into her purse. "That's over a hundred dollars. That's a good night's work for you."

"Doesn't matter," the girl said patiently, "my books get checked, just like the till. It all has to match up, or I get fired, and there'd be fifty people lining up to apply for my job. I'm sorry, I really am, but I can't take a chance. I got kids to support."

"So do I," Beth snarled. "Three of them, in that car out there, and if I don't get three gallons of gas, I can't give them a place to sleep tonight."

"So what," the girl snapped back, "do you think that's the first time I've heard that? Look around, lady, that's the world we're living in. Folks with nothing on the road going nowhere." She stepped back and leaned against the cigarette counter. Beth noticed that her light blue smock was stained and her name tag said, "Susan!" above the slogan, "Here to serve you!"

The girl rubbed her face, cupped her hands over her nose and mouth, and breathed deeply. Her eyes met Beth's and she said, "Look, I'm sorry. I'm sorry for your kids and I'm sorry for your situation. But my kids mean more to me than your kids do. I'm not gonna lose my job and let them go hungry just to get you another hundred miles down the road. The county has soup and sandwiches at the armory for folks like you, and a room full of cots. But I gotta warn you—they'll kick you out after two days, and when you get back in your car, the odds are someone will have siphoned out what's left of your gas. I don't think they'll let your kids starve, but there's a lot of things going on right now that I never thought would happen. It's a damn poor time to be on the road."

"I'm not on the road," Beth said, "I wish you'd stop saying that. I just need to get to Big Stone County. My people are there." That was a mild lie. Or perhaps a not-so-mild hope.

"Okay," the clerk said, "that's not so bad. You can get there. I'll even save you a few miles. When you go through Benson, don't get on Highway 12 to Ortonville. Instead go straight through until you get to Clontarf, then turn left." There was a road map of Minnesota under the glass countertop, and she traced the route with her forefinger, the nail half-covered with chipped black nail polish. "It's the only left, so you can't go wrong. It's a straighter road, saves you nearly 10 miles, but, you understand, there's not much traffic this time of year. You're not going to get any gas, not for any price. The gas all goes to the cities or to the farmers. The rest of us are just out of luck."

"Thanks," Beth said. "Thank you very much. I appreciate it." She took four strips of beef jerky and laid them on the counter. "What do I owe you?"

"Oh for Christ's sake," the clerk said. She grabbed a double handful of the jerky and shoved it into a bag. "We got bushels of that stuff. A dairy farmer outside of town, 5,000 cows, and he can't afford to buy feed anymore. He's been doing nothing but make jerky for the past month. The whole town is swimming in the stuff. You get back in your car and get where you're going. This is no time to be someplace where folks don't know you."

The kids were still asleep when she made the turn at Clontarf and headed across the prairie. Every now and then she could see a lonely yardlight, but they were few and far between and there was no traffic at all. They were heading for Steve's Great-Aunt Sharon's farm. They'd been there when Abby was four, but Aunt Sharon had gone into the nursing home the next year and died the year after that. The house and barns sat empty, and the farmland was rented out. She and Steve had planned to go there if things became untenable in the city, and she could only hope he'd find her there now. She'd been counting miles ever since Benson, keeping a running total in her head of how far she had yet to go. By her calculation, she was still twenty miles from the farm when the engine sputtered and died. The steering suddenly stiff in her hands, she coasted to a stop and pulled off onto the shoulder.

Abby stirred and sat up, looking around. "Mommy," she said, in a sleepy, puzzled, voice, "where are we?"

"Almost there," Beth said. "Remember, I told you we were going to the farm? Well, it's just down the road a bit. We might have to walk for a while, the car doesn't want to run right now."

"But it's cold, and it's dark, and I really have to pee."

"Right up there," Beth said, pointing toward a light gleaming on the horizon. "Right up there we can find a bathroom and someplace warm to sleep. And then in the morning we'll get to the farm and you can have chickens, and a dog, and maybe even a horse. How 'bout that?"

"Will you carry me?"

"No baby, I can't. I have the boys in their stroller and I have to carry a bunch of other stuff. You're my big girl and you just have to help."

Beth stepped out of the car and went to the trunk. The air was crisp and clear, with more stars than she'd ever seen gleaming above her head. She stopped for a moment and listened. Astonishingly, there was no sound. For a few moments she could hear nothing at all, and then, almost on cue, in the far distance she heard a coyote—the sound unmistakable even to her city-bred ears. Beth let the boys sleep while she unpacked the double stroller. The beef jerky and spare clothes were shoved in the stroller where a diaper bag should go, and finally, the pistol went in her pocket. The boys whined sleepily but soon settled down into their nests of blankets. Abby walked sturdily next to her. Beth shortened her stride so she wouldn't over-tire her. If Abby quit, Beth would be faced with choices she didn't think she could make.

"Who lives by that light, Mom?"

"I don't know, honey. But I bet there's a nice old lady there, and she'll give you a treat and let you sit by the fire. I bet her name is Agnes but she prefers to be called Grandma and her own grandchildren live in Tucson and she is lonely for children to spoil and fuss over."

Abby giggled. "Mom, you're just silly. I bet it's an old guy, and he's got a beard and one eye. He has a pet bear that sleeps under the kitchen table."

"Well, that's good, and that bear better watch his step, because I'm hungry enough to eat one. On the other hand, maybe the old lady's name isn't Agnes. Maybe it's Ludmilla, and she used to be a ballerina. She retired out here to the country because the lead dancer in the Bolshoi Ballet Company broke her heart in 1974. And if that's who it is, she'll serve us borscht."

"What's a borscht?" The conversation carried them two miles, but then it slowly trailed off.

There was no wind, no sound but their footsteps and the occasional squeak from a stroller wheel. Abby wasn't talking anymore—a bad sign—and Beth's shoulders ached from the weight of the pack. The yardlight slowly grew closer. Beth's spirits lifted when she was able to pick out the shape of a building. Her newest fear was that the light would have simply marked another group of steel grain bins, a bit of industrial agriculture holding no hope of refuge.

As they grew closer, the building grew taller, looming over the yardlight and obscuring what lay on the other side.

"Mom, what is it?" Abby asked, her voice very quiet and small.

"Oh," Beth said, "it's a church." They'd followed their light, their star, but it hadn't led them to a house, a home, with a nice gray-haired lady who would cluck over the children and bring them hot chocolate before tucking them into a bed under a thick quilt, where Beth could get a cup of coffee, a sandwich, and some sympathy. This was a dark, cold building next to a cemetery, and she didn't know what she was going to do.

They reached the parking lot and stopped. A wrought-iron sign to the left read, "Drywood Cemetery." It seemed a bleak name well suited for a harsh land. Beth slid the backpack off, sat on it, and buried her head in her hands.

It was a minute, no more, when she heard Abby. "Mom," she said, "Mommy , the door's unlocked."

Beth's head snapped up. She hadn't expected that. It took three trips up the stairs to get the boys and the stroller inside. Abby found a light switch inside the door, and the four stood together, looking around the small entryway. A note taped to a door caught Beth's eye.

"Welcome," it said, "If you are a traveler, there is some food in the kitchen in the basement and a few blankets and towels in the cupboard under the stairs. Please help yourself, take what you need, leave what you can, and tidy up as you depart. Our best wishes and prayers go out to you and your family in these difficult times."

Ten minutes later, Abby and the boys were drinking hot chocolate and eating peanut butter sandwiches made from slightly stale bread they'd found in the refrigerator. Beth sat on the floor, a blanket around her shoulders, and rubbed her feet. Lost in thought, she didn't notice when the kids' exploring turned instead to a raucous game of tag. It wasn't until she heard feet pounding up the stairs that she reacted.

"Hey, you guys," she yelled. "Get down here. Right now. Stay out of the sanctuary."

"Mom," Abby asked, "What's a sanctuary?"

"Well, a sanctuary is…" Her voice trailed off as she looked around the tiny church basement: the cheap wooden chairs and plastic tables from Walmart, the food and blankets waiting for lost and lonely strangers. The meaning of sanctuary swept over her, and she cried for a very long time.

She and her children made a nest of coats and blankets in one corner of the basement. The little boys were a warm and wiggly knot against her stomach, and Abby curled up against her back. Beth dropped off to sleep almost immediately and didn't stir when Abby left her side. At first, the sound of voices didn't penetrate her slumber, but as they went on, she slowly came to herself. It was Abby, and another voice, low and rumbling.

Beth's eyes popped open. As she rolled onto her back, she felt the shape of the pistol, hard and uncompromising against her skin. Panicked, she slid out from under the blankets and tiptoed up the stairs, just in time for the low voice to resolve into actual words.

"Sweetheart, are you here all alone?" It was a phrase from her worst nightmare, and she raced up the stairs, digging the pistol out of her back pocket. Turning the corner, she saw a man in heavy, dirty work clothes against the wall. He had a black stocking cap pulled down low over his forehead, and his hands looked big and strong.

"Don't you dare," Beth said. "I've got a gun."

There was sudden silence, a pause, and then the voice spoke again. "Good for you, darling. If my daughter were out and about in times like these, I'd hope she'd have a gun, too. Are you planning on doing anything in particular with the one you have?"

SO MUCH BOTHER

IT SHOULDN'T HAVE BEEN QUITE SO MUCH BOTHER. The three-point hitch on John's big tractor was malfunctioning, and the consensus opinion for the cause was a load-limit solenoid. It was a repair John could make himself, but he'd been to three dealerships looking for the part : starting in Milbank, heading to Madison, and finally going further east to Montevideo.

"C'mon, c'mon, c'mon," John said into his cellphone, cradling it against his ear while drinking vile coffee from a plastic cup. "I'll be there in twenty minutes. Can you keep someone there after hours? I've killed the whole afternoon on this, and it'll cost me a hundred bucks in gas to go home and come back over tomorrow. They're forecasting snow, and this is my snowblower tractor."

"Yeah, John, it's okay. Stop begging. I'll hang around myself. Just so I know you're coming for sure."

"Twenty minutes, a half hour tops. Thanks."

He was there in twenty minutes, but the part was hard to find— a design change in the middle of a model year, a serial number that didn't match up in the computer—and it was after 8:00 when he left the dealership. He stopped for a hamburger and then headed across the prairie for home. He turned onto County 22 and was on the last lonely stretch when he saw the tracks on the frosted highway.

The two sets of footprints weren't so unusual—people did walk for exercise, but not so many in the November dark. The other tracks were strange—as if they had a little cart or a sled they were pulling.

With nothing else to watch except a flat, straight road he'd seen a thousand times, he mulled over what had gone before him, trying various scenarios in his mind to fit the facts. The tracks turned into the old church by Drywood Lake and, despite the late hour, curiosity overwhelmed him and he wheeled his pickup into the parking lot to take a look.

He could see one light burning in the basement, which seemed odd, what with the cost of energy. He'd never seen a light on unless there were cars in the parking lot, but then there were those tracks.

It was late; he should be home, but these were curious times, and the mysterious tracks would drive him crazy if he just left them behind. He got out of the pickup and walked toward the church. A flicker of movement behind a basement window caught his eye as he climbed the stairs and opened the big door.

Inside the door, a double child's stroller filled the narthex. *Okay. That explains the tracks, but what the hell is someone doing out here pushing a couple of babies around?*

Light footsteps came up the stairs, and he waited quietly, his hands in his pockets. A little girl poked her head around the corner. Small and blond, with a dirty face and tousled hair, she stared at him solemnly. She looked worried. John tried to think of something reassuring to say. "You really scared me. If I believed in ghosts, I'd believe you are one. Are you a ghost, and are you going to haunt me?"

"I'm not a ghost," she said.

"Prove it," John said. "Say boo."

"Boo!" she said, giggling.

"Yeah, I believe you. You certainly don't sound like a ghost." To make himself smaller, he took a step backward and sat down on the floor. With a slight effort, he crossed his legs and leaned back against the wall.

"Sweetheart, are you here all alone!"

A rush of footsteps pounded up the stairs, and a tall blond woman burst into sight. Her clothing was in slight disarray and her hair was a mess. She waved a small pistol in his direction and said, "Don't you dare! I've got a gun!"

John looked at her, mildly puzzled as to her alarm. "Good for you, darling. If my daughter were out and about in times like these, I'd like to think she'd have a gun, too. Do you have any particular plans for the one you have?"

She stared, open-mouthed.

"My name is John," he went on, his tone quiet and even, calming and reasonable. "I saw your tracks and the light and stopped to see if everything was okay. I don't know where you're from, but in a lot of places, that would not be considered a shooting offense." He kept his voice low, trying to hide the pounding of his pulse under the threat. "Unless I'm missing something, it'd be okay with me if you pointed that thing in a different direction."

Beth looked down, flustered. She eased the hammer down and put her hand by her side. "I'm sorry. I woke up, and Abby was gone, and I heard your voice, and I…"

She stopped, not quite sure how to tell the stranger that she'd been about to kill him for being a backwoods pedophile.

John said, "It's okay. If we can agree that I'm not going to make any threatening moves and you're not going to shoot me unless I do, I think I'm going to stand up." He unfolded his legs and slowly rose. "What are you folks doing here, anyway? It's only Tuesday. It's a long time until Sunday services."

Beth gestured with the pistol. John winced when the muzzle passed in front of his face. "Back that way a couple miles, we ran out of gas. We're trying to get to Sharon Swenson's farm."

"Really," John said, "Sharon's been dead a couple years, and she was in the nursing home for five years before that. There's no heat, the electricity is turned off. What you planning to do there?"

"She was my husband's aunt. He's on a job in North Dakota, and we agreed to meet out here if things got too bad in the Cities. And, ah, now they are."

"So, you're—which one? Steve's wife?"

"You know Steve?"

"I knew him when he was four. I imagine he's changed some since." He looked at her, then at Abby, sighed, and appeared to make a decision. "Okay. Well, you can't stay here, but I can't just drop you off at an abandoned farm, either. My wife and I have a spare bedroom. Your kids could get a good night's sleep before you start the whole homestead thing."

"Excuse me?" she said. "I didn't ask for your help, and I certainly didn't ask for you to take over planning how my family is going to live."

"Okay," he asked, "what's your plan?"

He waited a couple of beats and then went on.

"There's a few things you should know," he said, his voice calm, level, and very quiet. "First, you don't know anything about guns, and it shows. I don't think you noticed, but you almost shot me by accident when you were pointing the way to your car. I'd hate to get shot by accident. Seems…tacky." He smiled, without a great deal of mirth. "Second, a lot of people around here do know a lot about guns, and they'll be able to tell just how clueless you are. Don't be pointing it at things you aren't planning on shooting." Beth took another step backward and put the pistol back in her pocket. "Plus, quite a few folks have spent a great deal of time working around things that can hurt you or make you dead. So, while that gun does buy you something, it might not have nearly as much stroke as you think it does."

He turned and walked to the window and looked out.

"We live in confusing times," he said. "Right now, I'm looking across the field and Thompson's yardlight isn't on. I've seen that yardlight my entire adult life. Ten years ago, maybe even a year ago,

I wouldn't even have thought a thing about it. But now I gotta wonder, did their electricity get turned off, did something burn out that couldn't be replaced, or did they just turn it off so people like you won't come wandering up?" He shook his head and came back to them. "I'm hoping we can shorten our conversation so there's a chance I can get home and get to bed. What d'ya think—can we load up your kids and get out of here? I don't know about you, but I've had a long day."

He was an inch shorter than her, and he was standing close enough that she could smell the faint odor of oil and exhaust fumes on his clothes. He had an intent, level gaze, and his face showed nothing but a mild interest in what she would say next.

"Mommy," Abby said, "Mommy, I'm still a little hungry, and I'm cold."

Beth said, "Why are you doing this?"

John laughed, "When you start piling out of my pickup, my wife is gonna welcome you in the house and then take me aside and say, 'What the hell were you thinking?' But if I just leave you here, she's gonna give me a wife look and she's gonna say, 'John, what the HELL were you thinking?'"

Beth took a deep breath. "Okay."

"There you go," John said. "Let's go find whoever belongs in that stroller and get out of here. I'm not exactly sure what I'm going to tell my wife, but that isn't really your problem. She might chew me out, but she won't hold it against you." He headed down the stairs and then turned to look at her again, a small smile in the corner of his mouth. "I'm guessing you don't really need to hear this, miss, but I gotta say, you really look like hell. I'm thinking it's been a long damn day for you, so I guess I'd recommend you sleep in tomorrow morning. You're too young to have bags under your eyes."

He turned to Abby. "Okay, kiddo, let's go find those babies. You help me out for another fifteen minutes and you can take the rest of the day off."

GOOD MORNING

BETH STRETCHED AND OPENED HER EYES. Her knees and feet ached from the day before. The room she was in was nearly dark, with a soft north light filtering through a small window. The ceiling and walls were plaster, with a few long cracks scattered randomly. The floor was of wide pine boards covered with scratched and faded gray paint. She turned her head at a muffled clank and gurgle in the corner and saw a big cast-iron radiator. The room was warm, almost too warm for the sheet and light blanket that covered her. It was a novel sensation—it was only November, but it felt like she'd spent her whole life shivering with cold toes and numb fingers. She was alone in the big iron bed, and she puzzled for a moment on how the kids could have gotten up without waking her, why they would have let her sleep, and why she wasn't worried.

The previous night was jumbled in her memory : crowding into the pickup as the farmer swept tools and parts off the passenger seat , a few minutes' drive with the twins squirming on her lap. Then, a big house with yellow light streaming out over the snow, a small woman greeting them at the door with a friendly smile and puzzled eyes. Half a cup of tea at a kitchen table and then a yawning stumble upstairs to the spare bedroom—all four of them in one bed and asleep in moments.

Beth stretched again, rotated her ankles, and felt a few small catches and cracks. She slid out of bed. Her jeans, shirt, and socks lay on the floor next to the bed. She pulled on her jeans and shirt, but after a look at her stained socks with a hole in the toe, headed downstairs in her bare feet.

She came down the stairs and found herself back in the kitchen. A young woman was sitting at the table, a magazine open and a baby busy nursing. She was dressed in sweatpants and a short silk robe. "Hey," she said with a merry smile, "you had a good sleep. Mom said a quick catch-up would be in order. I'm Sarah. Your kids are watching TV in the living room with about a bushel of Cheerios. My mom went to work and Daddy is out doing chores. He'll take you to fetch your car when you want it. He went over to your Aunt Sharon's place right away when he got up and left a note for your husband if he should show up. You got all that?" She nodded down at the baby and said, "This little monster is Emma." The baby grunted and sighed, right on cue. "I should have asked, can you carry on a conversation with my boob flapping in the breeze? I hope so, 'cause Emma eats about every three minutes. Daddy 'bout dies of embarrassment if he sees a flash of my skin, and if you're the same way, I'm gonna have to get myself a burka."

She stood up, shifted the baby to the other side, and padded over to the stove, turning on a burner under the tea kettle. "Just so you don't need to ask, I moved back home a couple months ago when my husband, the Noble Stan, decided dirty diapers and a lactating wife wasn't his American Dream, so he hit the road and I haven't the slightest freakin' clue where he went and I'm starting not to care."

"You're..." Beth paused for thought, "very open."

"Oh crap," Sarah said, "I'm one more bad relationship away from being a crazy cat lady. I got nothing to hide and I'm getting older by the second. Anything else you need to know?"

"I feel stupid," Beth said, "I don't even remember your parents' names."

"John and Amy. Mom is a special ed teacher, a pretty good cook, and the sweetest person on earth."

"And your father?"

Sarah shrugged. "Daddy is pretty much what he looks like. He's a farmer and he…does things, fixes things. Anything going on goes a little better when he's around. That may be a thing with the Noble Stan, 'cause Daddy can do anything and Stan pretty much hit his peak with the whole procreating thing. Although, girl to girl, he could procreate like a son of a gun."

"He scared me a little last night."

"Daddy? He's like the least scary person on earth." The kettle started to whistle, and Sarah got up and went over to turn off the stove. "Of course, you did pull a gun on him. He told us the whole thing at breakfast—makes a pretty funny story: 'The City Girl and the Revolver.' He wasn't mad, I can tell you that. He was maybe even a little proud of you for protecting your daughter against the ravaging hordes. Although, your judgment about who's a horde might need a little fine-tuning." She turned and flashed laughing blue eyes Beth's way. "I don't actually know what he would look like mad. I've never seen him beyond irked. Don't worry about him—he's a sweetie." She turned and looked Beth in the eye. "But, I gotta tell you, Daddy is Mr. Law and Order—does everything by the rules. But if you need it, really need it, he'll bury a body for you and he won't give you any shit about it after." She looked thoughtful. "Well, that's an insight I never had before—maybe that's why the Noble Stan headed for parts unknown." She looked in the cabinet to the left of the stove.

"We have jasmine or English Breakfast. Got a preference? I'm thinking a cup of tea and some toast. Then maybe you'll want to take a shower before you go get your car. Nothing personal, but you're a little smelly, and that observation is coming from a woman who does nothing but change diapers and wipe up vomit. You want to borrow some underwear?"

"I…have some, but thank you very much for the offer," Beth said.

WE'VE GOT A PLAN

BETH STEPPED OUT THE DOOR into a cold fog. The farm buildings around her were largely obscured, with a thick coating of frost on the trees and an otherworldly red sun gleaming in the far distance. There was a slight industrial hum to the air—unidentified motors doing unfathomable tasks. A half-dozen cats clustered around an ice cream pail full of scraps. Beth followed a row of dirty footprints that led down the sidewalk. The borrowed coat was heavy on her shoulders and redolent with the smells of straw and machinery, with an unsettling whiff of a man who was not hers.

Sarah had offered her some thick yellow chore gloves but laughed out loud when she'd tried them on. "I'm sorry," she said, "the oversize coat is sorta chic, in a lost-little-girl-on-the-prairie kind of way, but the gloves make you look like Mickey Mouse." Beth shoved her hands deeper into her pockets. She was wearing gloves, but they were leather driving gloves Steve had purchased for her at an open-air market in Florence during their last vacation Before. They were four years old now, showing their age, and not very warm.

A strong glow beat through the fog, and as Beth drew closer, she could see it was the lights of a greenhouse, tucked against the side of a much larger steel building. She found a door on the end and went in.

The floor of the greenhouse was several feet below ground level. Inside, the air was warm and wet. Rows of long plastic eavestroughs hung on wires, with greens and other vegetables at varying stages of growth. Beth's practiced eye took in a row of wilted plants. The air felt…wrong, and there was condensation on some plants that shouldn't be there. She poked a finger into one bed and frowned at the feel of too much moisture.

John was at the far end, planting something in a seed flat on a wooden table. He looked up and smiled. "Hey," he said. "I see you're up and about. Ready to go get your car?"

"Yes," Beth said, looking around. "This is great. How can you afford to heat and light it?"

"Well, let me show you," John said, pulling a coat and hat off a nail in the wall. "First, see the barrels in the back? Got them for free from the co-op. They're full of water and serve as kind of a heat sink, keeping the temperature a little more even." He motioned out the door and led the way to a small shed with a smokestack coming out the top. "Here's our wood boiler. It heats the water for radiators in the house, shop, and greenhouse. Insulated pipes run underground."

"What's that thing?" Beth asked, pointing at a squat metal object next to the boiler.

"That's a Stirling engine. I found a plan on the internet and a guy made it for me. I don't exactly know how to explain it, except it's a generator that just runs on one side being hot and the other side being cold. It's an old, old design—like 200 years old. It never caught on because there were other things more efficient. I've got some solar cells and a windmill, but on days like today, no sun and no wind, this is pretty much how we get our electricity. It's not very efficient, but since it pretty much just runs on waste heat, that isn't such a big deal."

"You mean you're off the grid?"

"Oh yeah. Basically, all three different generators dump their juice into a bank of batteries with a really good inverter." John opened the massive maw of the wood burner and threw in several logs. "Just for the sake of clarity, it's not really on purpose, it's 'cause the utilities don't get out here to fix our lines anymore when the juice goes out—we're just too far down on their list of worries. So, it just seemed simpler to not worry about them but fend for ourselves. I got a big grove, so if I cut a tree and plant a tree, I should be okay."

"That's amazing," Beth said.

"No," John said, "that's making do." He slammed the door on the furnace and turned to look at Beth, a crooked smile on his face. "It's kind of an acquired taste. You want to go get your car?"

In daylight, the landscape on the way back to her car seemed much less ominous. Flat farmland broken by lakes, sloughs, and small groves of trees. Abandoned farms outnumbered those that showed signs of occupancy. John and Beth sat high above the road in the big pickup.

"There's not much out here, is there?" Beth said, staring idly at the passing countryside.

"That's perhaps a matter of perspective," John said, "Last night there was a church." His tone was as quiet and level as always, but the reproof was clear and stinging.

Beth blushed, "I'm sorry. I didn't mean…" Her voice trailed off, unsure what to say next.

"No big deal," John said. "I'm maybe a little oversensitive about folks telling me there's nothing here. This is, you know, my home, but you'd be surprised at how easy it is for people to insult it." He shrugged and glanced her way. They drove in an uneasy silence for a few miles and then, out of the blue, he said, "You know, this country is kind of an acquired taste. It's not like the Rockies or the ocean. It takes a little time, a little patience. It's a hard land— let's face it, in a couple of months you'll be able to die just from going outside, and during July and August you won't die, but you might wish you had." He drummed his fingers on the steering wheel, choosing his words. "But this place is sort of like the grumpy uncle who nobody likes—the one who gets cigarette burns on the sofa and tracks mud into the living room, the one who doesn't like your cooking and thinks your kids are spoiled. But he's the guy you call if you need a loan, and he's the one who fixes the lawnmower and finds your dog when it gets lost."

He turned and looked at Beth, shrugged, and smiled shyly. "Am I making sense here? You're going to have to make up your own mind. We'll just get your car started and go from there."

He looked back at the road, frowned, and slowed as they descended a hill into a thick patch of fog. Beth kept looking at him, oddly drawn to this quiet, awkward man who'd so casually rescued her and her children and brought them into his home.

He asked, "Are you sure you ran out of gas?"

"Yes," Beth said. "Why?"

"Did you try to start it after it died?"

"Yes, a couple times. Why would that matter?"

"No problem. We'll get you home one way or the other. It's just that a lot of cars have their fuel pumps in the gas tank, and they're cooled by the gas in the tank. If you try to start the engine with no gas in the tank, sometimes it'll burn out the pump. And that means in this day and age you're screwed, because I don't know where you'd get the parts."

They drove by the church without slowing down, and Beth was surprised to see her car through the thinning fog almost immediately. "It seemed like we walked forever," she said.

"Scared, cold, and responsible for three little kids? You walked far enough."

Beth stared straight ahead. It seemed like faint praise, but she was surprised to feel a tear start down her cheek. It was a moment before she could find her voice. "Thanks," she said. "I keep trying to figure out what else I should have done. I just never thought of filling the tank while I was still in the Cities."

"Yeah, and what would you have done if you had gotten to Sharon's farm in the cold and the dark? The driveway is snowed in, there's no water, no heat. You did okay to get as far as you did and then you got a little lucky."

"What if you hadn't come along?"

John shrugged. "You would have slept on the floor and today someone would have stopped by. Out here, people watch things. I bet fifty bucks there'll be tire tracks by your car. Your kids might have gotten French toast for breakfast instead of Cheerios, but I'm pretty sure we wouldn't have let you freeze."

"You sure?"

"Pretty sure." John drummed his fingers on the steering wheel. "Although, the next 5,000 folks passing through might have it a little tougher. It'll take a while before it hits us out here that we're living in a different world."

He wheeled the pickup in a circle and pulled up in front of her car. He climbed out and pulled a gas can out of the box. "Let's hope your luck holds out."

Five minutes later, he gave up. "Not gonna happen," he said. "We'll move to Plan B." He took another gas can, some plastic tubing, and duct tape out of the pickup. "You're probably won't find this recommended in the owner's manual," he said, "but I was thinking about this while I was doing chores and I'm about 60 percent sure it will work."

He used the duct tape to fasten the gas can to the roof of the car. He ran the plastic tubing down inside the can and fastened it in place with another loop of tape. Beth watched wordlessly as his stained, clever hands moved quickly and surely.

"Aren't your hands cold?" she asked.

"Well, yeah," he said, "but I can't do this with gloves on. It's like the Eskimo story."

"What's the Eskimo story?"

"You must not have grown up in Minnesota, or else you had the worst father in the world. I had to sign a daddy oath to tell my kids the Eskimo story."

Beth laughed out loud, and then wondered how long it had been since she'd done that.

"Please," she said, "I would love to hear the Eskimo story."

"Okay. During WWII, when they were building the Alaskan highway, the regular construction workers would sit on the bulldozers for about 15 minutes and then have to come and get warm. Couldn't get anything done, so they tried hiring some local Eskimos to run the equipment. Those guys would just sit on that cold steel and work all day. They figured there must be some physiological difference, some way that the Eskimos had adapted to the cold over the centuries, so they brought in a bunch of scientists to do experiments to figure out what it was."

"Is this true?"

"Doesn't matter. It could be true. Never let the truth get in the way of a good story. Anyway, do you know what they found out? There was no physiological difference at all. The difference came from the fact that the regular workers were cold and wanted to be warm. And if you're sitting on a bulldozer in Alaska in the winter, that won't happen. The Eskimos were just as cold, but they knew that if they were going to get anything done, that was just part of the deal." He turned to look at her, making certain she got the point. "It's not about whether you're cold or not—it's about not caring."

He pulled a folding knife from a sheath on the left side of his belt, fumbled it open one-handed, and cut the tubing to length.

"Here we go," he said. "I think we're in business. You see, all the fuel pump does is get the gas up to the engine. Gravity might work just as well." He fed the tube under the hood and inside the engine compartment. "Now comes what we in the biz refer to as 'the icky part.'" He took a deep breath, exhaled into the tube, and then inhaled sharply. He gagged, spit out a mouthful of gasoline, and stuck the end of the tube, with gas running freely out the end, onto a barbed fitting. "Try and start it now." The engine turned over, coughed, and sputtered to life.

"How 'bout if I drive your car? It might be a little tricky keeping it going." John opened the car door, and Beth obediently climbed out.

She asked, "How did you know this would work?"

He slid behind the seat, rolled down the window, and said, "I didn't. But I've run out of gas enough times that I've tried most every other way I could think of. Now let's see if this thing blows up."

He put the car in gear. It stalled, sputtered, caught again, and headed west.

Beth watched for a moment and then clambered up into the pickup and followed. The fog had lifted by now, and the landscape was exposed to examination. The farms had a put-away look—crops harvested, machinery shedded, and the land turned. Exposed roots clawed out of the black ground, and small drifts of dirt dappled windblown snow filled the crannies and hollows of the fields. Ruined and abandoned farms occurred every mile, nestled in run-down groves with old machinery and junk piles peering through the underbrush and toppled trees. Far less common were occupied farms—giant grain bins, huge new houses, with an occasional combine or four-wheel-drive tractor too large to fit in a building parked proudly in the yard.

The land looked harsh and abandoned, until Beth started in surprise as one particularly rugged field erupted as thousands of Canadian geese, fortuitously evolved to blend into disturbed farmland, took to the air. A half mile further, she had to slam on the brakes to avoid a rooster pheasant that, like a feathered Frisbee, sailed across the road three feet in the air and then flailed its tail feathers, stalled, and dropped gently down, disappearing into a patch of cattails. Blood smeared the highway, and the corpse of a whitetail deer lay on the shoulder of the road where it had been dragged after its early-morning collision with a pickup truck.

The sky went on forever. On the far horizon, Beth could see the outlines of a dozen massive wind turbines, spectral blades slowly churning the morning air, but they were the only signs of human life and industry.

Ahead of her, John turned off the main road and she followed. She puzzled for a moment, then realized he was headed for Aunt Sharon's farm.

He stopped on the road and waited for her by the car. The driveway already had a small snowdrift across it. Beth walked up to him and looked around. There were no neighboring farms visible. John had stuck a shovel in the snowdrift and taped a note to the handle.

"Steve," it read, "your wife and kids are safe and at my place. John. Three miles west, one north."

Beth said, "Is that it? I'm not moving in with you. I don't even know you."

"Okay," John said, "We'll get your car home. We'll get it fixed. You'll go someplace, get a job, save some money, find a place to live, and then you can come back and change the sign. How's that sound?" His voice was bland and even, but Beth sensed a note of irritation that matched her own.

She turned her back on him and examined the small frame farmhouse in front of her. The paint was peeling and it looked like an attic window was broken. The other time she'd been here was in the summer, and then it had looked quaint and fun. Now it looked lonely and abandoned, dangerous and decrepit.

"I checked this morning," John said, "it has an old fuel oil furnace and the tank is empty. It would cost about $3,000 to fill the tank, and I'm not completely certain that the co-op is taking on any new customers, even if they pay cash. The rural electric—I don't know; we'd have to ask. This is the last house on this mile and the juice has been shut off for a couple years—I don't know if the lines and transformers are still working or not."

Beth nodded and looked around, appraising.

"One thing I don't understand," she said. "Why was the church unlocked last night?"

John came up and stood beside her. "It always seemed to me, that if you can't get into the sanctuary, it isn't really much of a church. But that's just my opinion." He leaned on the shovel, pushing it further into the snow. "It's not my church, but I'm guessing it's never been locked—maybe they can't even find the key."

He turned and looked at her. "You are right, though. You don't know me. And I don't know you. And fitting another four people into a house that already has a couple of spares wouldn't be my first choice. I wouldn't want you to tell all those feminists I live with, but if you were a man, and alone, I'd buy you a tank of gas and wish you well. But you're a woman, with three little kids and not many options, and I'm afraid that we're maybe all just stuck in a situation none of us want to be in. So what's it going to be? Amy and Sarah and I talked it over this morning. Unless you have other plans, you can stay with us until Steve shows up or you can come up with a Plan B of your own. I have to warn you though: you'll be eating lots of beans."

Beth laughed, "Beans, huh. I can tell you about beans."

"Really," John said, "grow up poor, did you? Eat more beans than you cared to remember?"

"No," Beth said, "I did my PhD work on biodiversity in edible beans."

"No shit," John said, "you're an honest to God doctor?"

"I'm a doctor," Beth said, "and I'm honest. But these days, I'm not sure where God enters into it."

"Well, I wouldn't argue with you." He took a deep breath of the chill morning air. "But then, you did find a church last night. There's that."

Beth laughed and looked him up and down. "Do you know who Freeman Dyson is?"

"A science dude, right?"

"Well, yeah, you could say that. He once said something about how a bird flying high in the sky sees the full scope of the world, while a frog nestled in the mud only sees the beauty of the flower right next to it. It isn't that how the bird sees is better or more important than what the frog sees, it's just a different point of view. Do you suppose you could get this frog out of the cold and back to her children? That's what I need to see right now."

"Okay," John said.

"And," she added, "your greenhouse is messed up. You're getting gray mold because the humidity is too high. I don't know anything about fuel pumps, but I know I can fix your greenhouse."

On the drive back to John's farm, Beth noticed a faint orange streak across the clear blue sky, trailing for many miles with the prevailing wind, and resolved to ask John what it was. But when they arrived, Abby rushed out to tell her that she'd gone to gather eggs all by herself while Sarah watched the boys, and a rooster had pecked her, and then they'd made an egg sandwich. She gathered her into her arms and all thoughts of birds, frogs, and strange orange streaks left her mind for the time being.

IN THEORY...

THEORETICALLY, the highest storm surge possible was supposed to be 38.5 feet in New Bedford, Massachusetts. New Bedford was chosen as an example because it was at the end of a narrow bay that could act as a funnel in a Category 4 hurricane.

As it turned out, the theory was wrong. Sea levels were rising too fast to reset the benchmark—after all, the Petermann Glacier alone contributed a foot of rise. Plus, there was never supposed to be more than a Category 4 hurricane, which was optimistic as well. Winds of 190 mph and 43 inches of rain meant the storm surge cleared 40 feet, easy. Because the storm was so massive, sweeping down the entire East Coast, there really was no chance of evacuating. Where do you put nearly 100 million people? They called it a bomb cyclone, because it happened in the winter, but no one knew how fast it would intensify. Experience had shown that there was a 3.9% increase in 90 day mortality when evacuating vulnerable populations, just from the shock of moving. Nobody wanted that, so the recommendation was to shelter in place.

Which was kind of a pity.

With all the deaths, it took a while to notice, but when the refineries in New Jersey, Philadelphia, and Savannah were ruined, another 2 million barrels a day of what ran the country just went away. It took even longer for people to wonder what had been in all those miles of chemical processing plants that lined the water in New Jersey. After the storm, many of those tanks were broken and empty, with their contents leaking into the aquifers and watersheds. It was a problem that eventually would go away.

Of course, it might take a thousand years.

If the people in Washington had any last words, no one heard them.

Perhaps no one was listening.

YOU'RE GONNA HATE IT

JOHN WAS STANDING in line at the grocery store when Bobby sidled up behind him and whispered in his ear.

"I hear you're starting your own little harem out there on the ranch."

John didn't turn around but said, quietly enough so the teenage girl running the till couldn't hear, "If I want any shit out of you, I'll squeeze your head."

Bobby giggled and said, "You got time for a cup of coffee?"

"Yeah," John said, "if you're buying."

"Hey, I'll get you a cup of coffee *and* a cookie, if you'll tell me the story about how you keep accumulating house guests."

"Well, the short version is, it's not on purpose."

"I want the long version."

"You always do. It's because you don't have a job—you got time for long stories."

The café was long and narrow , with plastic-covered booths, oilcloth tablecloths, and a high tin ceiling encrusted with a century of grease and nicotine. Bobby grabbed two cups of translucent brown coffee and joined John at a booth next to the big cracked picture window in the front.

"So what's the scoop? They say you got a big, beautiful blond woman out there."

John snorted. "Well, yeah, along with her three kids and Sarah and Emma. Remember Sharon Hendrickson? She died a couple years ago and lived east of me?"

"Yeah, on that little place south of 22?"

John took a sip of coffee and said, "There you go. Anyway, her nephew Steve married this woman and then took off to find work, and she got laid off and she decided she'd become a pioneer woman. Except it's the middle of November, that house is unlivable, and she's got no money."

"I'm following you so far, except for the part where they all move in with you."

"That part's a little hazy to me, too."

"So, you're in town buying groceries and all the women folk are laying around watching Oprah."

"No, Sarah's got the kids whipped into shape—she just sits around holding Emma and shouts orders, and the woman, Beth is her name by the way, has been fixing up the greenhouse."

"Yeah? Did she work for a nursery?"

"Oh, hell no. She's a college professor. She worked on the St. Paul campus until the governor cut the budget. She didn't have tenure, so they just said, 'See ya,'"

"What's Steve doing?"

"I don't know for sure, and neither does she. He's an engineer, went out to the oil fields out the other side of Bismarck, but then he called her on his cell phone and told her he was going someplace else, except the reception was crapola, like it is in that part of the country, and then they were disconnected and that's all she's heard for about a month."

"Jesus," Bobby said.

"Well, exactly. She runs out of money, they're going to disconnect her heat, and so she saddles up and heads for the farm to live off the land."

"Except, of course, it's November and she's got no heat and no food." An unthinkable story a few years previously, now all too common.

"Except for that, yeah."

Bobby went over to the counter and brought back a pot of coffee and topped off their cups.

"How's the greenhouse out at the recycling center going?"

"I don't know, Bobby. I'm not a county commissioner anymore, remember? It's not my problem."

"Well, what I hear is that it's pretty much shut down except for a couple pots of geraniums. Nobody wanted to mess with it, so they're just burning the garbage and letting the heat go up the stack."

"Like I said, Bobby, not my problem."

"Maybe. But maybe you could just swing by there and see if they could use any help. You watching the news lately? It might be nice to have some lettuce growing before they decide that they can't afford diesel fuel to ship produce out here in the sticks. It's a long time till spring if we're all living on corn muffins and beef jerky."

"Hey, I'm nobody, remember?"

"Yeah, just the guy who saw this coming."

"No, I'm not. I never dreamed some idiot would blow up half our oil."

Bobby snorted impatiently, "You saw things going south, and you did what you could to get this whole county ready for it. You know that, and so do I. It's getting so more and more of the folks around here are seeing it, too. Go out to the greenhouse, look around. If you make a suggestion, they'll listen to you, and you know they will. What have you got to lose? Your house is full of little kids. You got no reason to go home anytime soon anyway."

John met his gaze and then looked down at his cup. "This is still the worst coffee in the world, isn't it?

"Yeah," Bobby said, "pretty much. It's weak, but at least it's stale."

A truck rumbled by outside. They watched it go, a small plume of snow rising off the back tires. John said, "Have you noticed how there are more people around? Kids visiting their parents and grand-parents, and just hanging around. Does that mean something?"

"It means they got nothing else to do, and some of them got nowhere else to go," Bobby said. "Are you planning on answering my question?"

"How come you don't do it? You're rich. People must think you know something."

"Because I'm a fuckup who got lucky," Bobby said. "Every-body knows that."

"What if I'm not so sure that's true?"

Bobby wrapped both hands around his coffee cup and looked up. "Then you can just keep your mouth shut."

John snorted and then yelled across the room, "Lisa, Bobby said he'd buy my coffee. Don't let him sneak out without paying. And I'm leaving a tip, a big one. Make sure he doesn't stiff you."

An elderly woman with pin curls and wearing red sneakers poked her head out of the kitchen, waved an arm and said, "Got it, John. Thanks for the heads-up."

John headed for the door.

Bobby said, "Hey, you didn't leave a tip."

John said, "Who's she gonna believe? Me or you?"

And then he was gone.

♦　♦　♦

The greenhouse was a mess. The air was warm and dry but smelled stale. Two forlorn flats of herbs sat on the floor next to the office door. John opened the door and looked in.

"Hey Oscar," he said, "what's up?"

"Hey John." Oscar looked up from his desk. Oscar had red hair, cut high and tight, and the muscles in his cheeks looked like he was

134

storing walnuts. At 5'10" and 145 pounds, he was all sharp edges and hard corners. He was wearing blue jeans and a faded T-shirt with a Leatherman riding high on his belt on the left side. As he stood up John noticed that after five years out of the Marines, he was still wearing his combat boots, and John even saw the slight gleam of dog tags laced into the right boot. John reached out his left hand. The handshake was warm and firm, and he could feel the rasp of Oscar's calluses against his own.

"How's your hand coming?"

Oscar held up the remnants of his right hand—a tangled, shiny red mass of scar tissue with a thumb and a nubbin of a finger coming out of the middle.

"It's okay. That toe they transplanted kind of works like a thumb, but not really. I can tie my shoes and open a beer, and really, what else is there?" He shrugged. "I'm pretty much off the painkillers now, so that's a good thing."

"How come you're not using the greenhouse? I just had coffee with Bobby at the café, and he told me it was shut down."

"Jeez, John, that shit'll kill you. They shouldn't even be allowed to call it coffee."

"Hell, Oscar, they're Lutherans. They should know how to make coffee."

"Oh bullshit." Oscar leaned over in his chair and flipped the switch on a hotplate. "Sit down. I'll make you some real coffee. They all talk about egg coffee and this and that, and then they use the cheapest buck-a-pound decaf they buy at Walmart. They don't know shit. You gotta start with good beans. After that, it's kind of hard to fuck up." He set a small wok on top of the hotplate and poured some pale beans into it. As the aroma filled the room, he leaned back in his chair and occasionally stirred the roasting beans with a cut-off golf putter.

"If you want good coffee, you can use Jamaican Blue Mountain Number One, or Kona is pretty good too. Colombian don't mean shit—it's just good advertising. Personally, though, I roll with Ethiopian Yirgocheffe. That's what coffee is supposed to taste like." When the beans were properly black, he used an old tube sock as a hot pad and tipped the wok full of beans into a grinder, while putting what looked like a small cast-iron teapot with a tall neck on the hotplate. "Good beans and good water and you're almost there. Of course, you need to use a burr grinder instead of blades—makes all the difference in the world."

When the water was hot, he measured four tablespoons of coffee into the pot. "There we go. Four minutes and we got coffee. You want to grab some cups out of the cupboard?"

John followed his nod and found some delicate porcelain cups in the top of a beat-up plywood cabinet. "Someday you might have to tell me how you learned how to make coffee like you're in some village in Ethiopia."

Oscar chuckled. "I'd have to check the statute of limitations first. But I can tell you why the greenhouse is sitting empty. Nobody wanted to piss around with it, mainly. I'm pretty much busy running the recycling and burner, and the county cut the budget, so we had to lay off the interns. The grocery stores said they could get the stuff cheaper someplace else, and nobody wanted to peddle vegetables from under an umbrella. The greenhouse stays warm all the time 'cause of the exhaust from the burner, but I've shut off the ventilation and all the other crap."

John nodded, leaned back against the wall, and tucked his heels under the rung of his chair. He emptied his cup, straining out a few grounds with his teeth. He set the cup down, laced his hands behind his head, and yawned.

Oscar put his feet up on the gray metal desk.

"You know," John said, "have you noticed all the new people around?"

"Well, yeah. People getting laid off and moving home with their folks or granny." He shrugged. "Hard time, John, hard times. I'm sure glad I'm not sitting around watching 'Judge Judy' with my mom. It'd drive me out of my freakin' mind."

John nodded. "So tell me, how many guys did you boss around when you were in the Corps?"

"I dunno. When I was a gunny, I suppose fifty or so. Of course, I wasn't the platoon leader, but the lieutenant was a freakin' moron. Why do you ask?"

"Oscar, I got a plan, and you're going to love it."

Oscar frowned. "Are you sure about that?"

"No," John said, "In fact, you'll pretty much hate it. But it's important, and it's the right thing to do."

"Well, that's probably close enough. Let's hear it."

CHINESE TSUNAMI

THEY CALLED IT THE CHINESE TSUNAMI, but it had nothing to do with a tidal wave.

Lao Baixing in Chinese means, literally, "Old One Hundred Names." It refers to the fact that there are so few surnames in China, a billion people share the same 100 names. Like most peasants, they are remarkably peaceful, wanting only to raise their children and live out their lives without attracting the attention of the government. But every few hundred years, the people in charge do something so unforgivable that even a peasant's patience can be exhausted.

And that's when the dynasties change.

It started in Inner Mongolia, near the town of Baotou.

In 1958, a state-owned company, the Baotou Iron and Steel Company, began processing rare earth elements there. By the 21st century, 97% of the rare earth minerals produced in the world came from China. It's not that China is the only place they're found; it's that the pollution from refining them was so extreme that no one else wanted to pay the environmental cost. But China didn't care.

Zhang Ju had one child, a son, and he died before his third birthday from thyroid cancer. Her neighbor three houses down lost her daughter a month later. The people who ran the refineries didn't care, nor did the inspectors paid to look the other way, nor did the government officials who shared in the profits. But the mothers—

the mothers cared a lot. They talked to each other and then talked to their neighbors.

Zhang Ju and her neighbor died in some of the first protests, shot down by police charged with keeping the peace. They were some of the first. No one really knew who were the last, because the news stopped coming out of China long before the smoke from the burning factories stopped.

In a matter of weeks, the world started to run out of a lot of stuff that it didn't even know it needed.

A LOT OF MEAN

IT WAS COLD. Bobby drove down the gravel road under a December sky—light blue with wisps of cirrus scudding south, driven by a hard wind out of the north. He bounced over small snowdrifts and wove between the bigger ones. Since the gas shortage, the county had stopped plowing roads unless they were impassable with a four-wheel drive *and* on a bus route. Everyone else stayed home or walked. He turned into John's driveway, which was plowed clean and wide just as usual. A thin plume of smoke rose from the shop, and there was an extra vehicle in the yard : a gleaming red '66 Chevy pickup, with chrome wheels, two tall chrome stacks, and a Marine Corps sticker in the rear window. Bobby pulled up and parked behind it just as John came out of the greenhouse carrying a paper bag full of lettuce.

"Hey," Bobby said, nodding toward the pickup, "what's Oscar doing out here?"

"Fighting with the women. I got sent to get some greens for lunch, and I was glad to go."

They walked together toward the house. John's usually immaculate farmyard looked like a war had been fought across it—the snow was stamped into intricate patterns, and there were several deep yellow-rimmed holes melted in the snow. Bobby nodded toward one of them. "Did you get a dog?"

"Oh hell no," John said, wry disgust in his voice, "one of those little boys is just excited as hell at the novelty of being able to pee outside. It's apparently great entertainment."

Bobby laughed out loud.

"This is good for you," he said, "loosens you up a little."

"Ya think? I don't know, I thought I had just plenty of chaos in my life already. Are you feeling lonely? A couple of them could move in with you."

"Thanks for the offer," Bobby said, "but I'm pretty sure I don't have room. The cat has moved back in, and I'm thinking of getting a puppy. I just don't think I could cram any more people in that house."

"Tough," John said, "you lead a tough life. You hang in there, buddy."

They entered the house and added their coats and boots to the pile by the door. As John opened the door to the kitchen, a blast of warmth and raised voices came through. Sarah was the first one to look up. When she saw Bobby, she leaped to her feet, ran, and jumped into his arms. "I've been thinking about it," she said in a sultry whisper. "You can stop begging. I will run away with you to Tahiti. Daddy can take care of Emma, and it'll just be you and me on a beach eating coconuts." She lowered her voice further. "Like you said, I'm not packing any clothes."

Bobby turned an anguished eye toward John. "Will you please," he said, "get your daughter off me?"

John gave what could only be described as a growl and hooked one arm around Sarah's midsection, peeled her off Bobby, tucked her under his arm, and carried her, flailing her pink cowboy boots, back to the kitchen table.

Oscar had been looking on with vast amusement and then said, "As I was saying, now that we're cranking out tomatoes and lettuce, what are we going to do with it all?"

John shrugged, "The people who work get it for free. The people who can't work get it for free. The people who won't work pay through the nose or starve."

"Really, Daddy?" Sarah said. "Isn't that a little old school?"

"Skin in the game, baby," John said. "We need to get people feeling like they're part of something, because once you have an investment, you'll work to protect it."

"Your dad is right, Sarah," Bobby said. "Right now, people are letting us do what we want because they know your dad and no one has a better idea. But the town is filling up with strangers, and we need to make them part of the team, the faster the better, because sooner or later someone is going to show up with an alternative plan for the future. Which might be wonderful, might be terrifying. Either way, we want people on our side. When Dean Smith was at North Carolina…"

Sarah interrupted, "Who is Dean Smith?"

Beth said, "The guy who taught Michael Jordan how to play basketball."

It was the first thing she'd said, and Bobby locked eyes with her briefly before he went on, "Well, that's perhaps his *condensed* résumé, but close enough. Anyway, when one of his players committed a technical foul in a game, he'd just go nuts, because a technical foul is nothing more than lack of self-discipline and selfishness. Just drove him nuts. So, at the next practice, he'd take the player who'd committed the foul, have him sit in a lawn chair in the middle of the court and drink a Coke, while the rest of the team ran wind sprints until they were exhausted."

"That's just mean," Sarah said.

"It's the same thing the Corps would do," Oscar said.

"Just because it's what a bunch of bloodthirsty barbarians would do doesn't mean it's right for us," Sarah said, "No offense, Oscar."

Oscar shrugged. "I didn't even know that was an insult."

Bobby said, "Say what you will about Oscar's former col-leagues in the break-things-and-kill-people biz, they're the best. So, you've got the best basketball coach ever and the best military group ever using the same techniques for building a team. We should prob-ably give it a think. We want people feeling good about helping and we want them resenting the ones who don't help."

"That's mean, too," Sarah said.

"Baby," John said, "I'm afraid there's going to be a lot of mean from here on out. No help for it. We just need to make sure we don't start liking it."

◆　◆　◆

The house was finally quiet. John and Amy lay close together, relishing the silence. With the house full of people and half of them children, their time alone in bed was strictly limited, with 2:00 a.m. nightmares often leading to one or two small bodies squeezing in with them.

John lay flat on his back, cataloging all that was wrong with his body, from his aching arches to his bad left knee, up to the persistent pain when he turned his head and, most worrisome, what felt like a chipped left middle molar. Beth was curled around him, soaking up his body heat after a long day in an old school with the heat turned down to 63.

"This is nice," John said.

"Yeah, but only until you start to snore. Then the evening goes south." John snorted. After a moment, Amy continued, "So, our new boarder, she's got a few quirks."

"Yeah, well, what's your point? Have you talked to our daugh-ter lately? This house is full of quirky. Beth has three little kids, the world is falling apart, her husband is missing, and she's living with a bunch of people she barely knows. I think a few quirks are under-standable."

"Solid points, but have you noticed that when she's stressed, she mumbles?"

"What the hell, Amy?"

"No, it's like a chant or something, and her eyes glaze over. She worries me."

"Worry like you're not sure she washed her hands after going to the bathroom, or worried she's gonna boil a bunny?"

"Halfway between."

"She's really smart. That greenhouse went from nothing to feeding about half the county."

"Hey, I'm not saying she isn't smart. She's smart, friendly, helpful, all that."

"But quirky."

"Well, that may not be the right word. But there's something there."

"Yeah, I know. I'm not going to ask her about it."

Amy laughed. "John, come on, have you ever, I mean, ever, asked anyone anything? You live in constant fear that you'll find out something personal about someone and be forced to deal with it. For a guy who's so good at so much, you suck at being human. No offense."

"None taken. I think."

"Seriously, though, if that young woman were a kid in my class, I'd never, and I mean never, take my eye off her, because she's strung pretty tight."

"I'll add her to the list of things I'm going to worry about. It could be a while before a spot opens up. Right now I'm worried about that shirt choking you in the night. You should probably take it off."

"Yeah, get back to me on that in May when I stop shivering."

A few moments later, John did start to snore. Amy nudged him onto his side and wrapped herself even closer. After a while, she fell asleep, too.

Just not right away.

THERE USED TO BE FOUR

BETH STRAIGHTENED HER TIRED BACK. The greenhouse was warm and moist, and all around her, she heard the hum of conversation as people plucked and weeded, watered and planted, trading their labor for some fresh vegetables. Most days she enjoyed the contact, but for some reason, today felt crowded.

She slipped on her coat and exited into the cold Minnesota winter.

Oscar was there, squatting on his heels and staring at the stub of a cigarette in his hand.

"Hey," she said.

"Hey," he replied, squinting up at her. "So, what am I going to do when they run out of tobacco?"

"Live longer and smell better."

"Well, there's that."

She stretched again, pressing her hands hard against her kidneys and rotating her shoulders.

"I've been wondering," she said, nodding toward the west, "what's that streak of orange and yellow you see in the sky every now and then?"

Oscar followed her nod, "Oh, that's the plume from the power plant. Dumbest thing ever. When they were building it about 50 years ago the locals didn't want it in the county because they thought it would ruin their view. So it ended up in South Dakota. South

Dakota gets all the property taxes plus we're downwind of the smokestack so we get all the pollution, too. *And* it ruins the view."

Beth froze, like a cat spying a snake. "What? What's in it?"

Oscar shrugged. "The usual, I suppose : sulfur, mercury, carbon dioxide, and a few other things. This winter it's been worse than usual. My guess is no one is worried about pollution anymore; they just want to keep the lights on. Plus, what are the chances someone from Washington is going to come out and check? Pretty damn slim. I wouldn't be surprised if they've just unhooked all the pollution control equipment and are just running straight pipes out of the boiler. Who's gonna tell them not to?"

"So that's what we're breathing. That's what we're all breathing! But we're out in the country; the air's supposed to be clean out here."

Oscar looked up, surprised by her sudden urgency. "You'd think so, but the people in charge like to put dirty stuff in places where there aren't enough people to complain. We need jobs and we don't have any clout. So, yes, that's what we're breathing."

He was stunned by her transformation. Her face was deadly pale, except for red spots high on her cheeks. Her hands were trembling as she stood and paced, a few steps one way and then the other.

"But that's not right. That can't be. We can't have that." Her voice rose, turned staccato. "There used to be four, but that was before. There used to be four, but that was BEFORE!"

Oscar stood, grabbed her by the shoulders, and said, "Hey, kid…"

Beth kicked him hard in the knee and brushed him aside. The closest vehicle was Oscar's shiny red pickup, and the keys were in it. Oscar was bent over, squeezing his kneecap between both hands when he heard his pickup start up. He looked up in time to see the back end fishtailing on the gravel until, with a shriek of rubber, it hit the tar road and headed south. He clawed his phone out of his pocket.

Cell service had been spotty for months, but today there were three bars. He paused for thought and then dialed John.

"Hey, John," he said.

"What's the matter, Oscar? You sound funny."

"Yeah, well, your girlfriend just beat me up and stole my pickup."

"What? What? What the hell are you talking about?"

"Beth. She just slipped a cog. She asked me about the smoke from the power plant, and when I told her, she just slipped a cog. It's a long story, John, but she took my pickup and she's driving eighty miles an hour toward the power plant. No shit, John, you better do something."

"What?"

"Stop saying that! Get your head out of your ass and find her. Whatever set her off, she's stuck on crazy and turned up to 11."

The phone went dead, and John stared at it for a moment. *When did this become my problem?* passed through his mind, but he climbed in his pickup and turned south. He'd known Oscar for thirty years and had never heard him sound excited—until now.

His house was five miles closer to the power plant than the greenhouse, but the woman had a head start on him and it sounded like she was driving faster than he would. He floored the accelerator, but his right foot was the only part of his body that wanted to be there.

KILLING THE POWER

BETH DROVE SOUTH ON HWY 75, her mind a screaming frenzy—nothing coherent except a raging refrain of "There used to be four, but that was before," repeating over and over. Traffic was sparse—gasoline was both rare and expensive, and with the onset of winter, most people just stayed home. She met only two cars in eleven miles and blew through the stop sign in Ortonville without pause. She crossed the bridge into South Dakota, and as she came up the hill, the smokestack from the power plant dominated her vision. This close, there appeared to be no exhaust visible. It was only when the superheated effluent cooled that the faint trace of orange and yellow appeared. She followed the grid of roads, taking lefts and rights, gradually getting closer. The entire huge complex finally came into view, and for just a moment, her scientific brain kicked in. What was she going to do? How could she damage this massive artifact enough to shut it down? She had no idea what was inside a power plant, let alone what was vital and irreplaceable. Her eye fell on the barbed wire enclosure full of transformers. This was a vulnerable target, and she aimed the pickup that direction.

The old pickup's manual transmission was no problem for Beth, although considerably clunkier than the sports cars she'd driven. The lack of power steering is what betrayed her. She was shifting gears when the left front wheel hit a massive pothole and jerked the steering wheel out of her loose grasp. The truck bounced once, twice, and came down with the front wheels cranked hard to the right. They caught on the scuffed asphalt, and the truck pinwheeled three times before coming to rest upright a few feet away from the fence guarding the transformer farm. Beth sagged into the seat belt, blood dripping from her nose and sparks of pain from a broken finger shooting up her arm. She dimly felt hands fumbling with her seat belt and then heard the snick of a knife opening. The belt fell away and strong hands pulled her from behind the wheel.

"Come on, kid," John said, "this is a…spectacular mess, and we better get the hell away from it."

Beth felt his arm around her waist as he dragged her away from Oscar's pickup and she heard his grunt of effort as he lifted her into his. Then she didn't hear anything at all.

♦　♦　♦

The smell brought her around.

She had a brutal headache, along with various other pains. Even blinking hurt, but after a few seconds, her vision cleared. She was sitting in John's pickup. He was next to her, his seat reclined several notches as he sipped a cup of coffee. Another cup sat in the cupholder by her left elbow. She picked it up and took a sip of her own.

"Bobby says," John said, "that coffee needs to grow at high altitudes within 500 miles of the equator and there's no place like that in the continental United States. What's going to happen when we run out of coffee and can't get more?"

Beth closed her eyes, took a long drink, and leaned back. "Strictly speaking, that's not true. Coffee shrubs need a warm, humid climate with lots of diffused light and about 100 inches of rain a year. You can grow it in a greenhouse. No one does it because it's not economically viable when you have peasants all over the world willing to work on coffee plantations for a dollar a day."

"Okay then," John said, "one less thing to worry about. Which reminds me…" he fumbled his phone out of his pocket and made a

150

call. "Hey, Oscar," he said, "would you please call the cops and tell them that when you came out of the greenhouse, your pickup was missing."

He paused for a few seconds and then said, "Because I said please." He listened again and then said, "Thanks, Oscar. When they find your pickup, it might need a few scratches buffed out. You can use my shop if you want." He hung up the phone and took another sip.

Beth said, "I suppose you want an explanation."

John laughed, "If my wife were here, she'd think it's pretty funny that you know so little about what I want and don't want. No, I don't want an explanation, but I guess I should find out if this is going to happen very often."

Beth nodded, "What do you know about spina bifida?"

"Well, not much, except it typically doesn't have anything to do with stealing pickup trucks."

"You think this is funny?"

"Listen, kid, about twenty times a day I have to make a conscious choice between laughing and crying. I'm not saying I always make the right choice. Keep going."

"So, when Abby was a year old, I got pregnant again. It was sort of an accident. I was working on my doctorate, my husband was just getting rolling in his career, we hadn't had a night's sleep in about a year and a half…just bad timing all around. Anyway, it was another little girl. We named her Summer, and she was wonderful, except for the spina bifida. It was the worst kind: meningomyelocele, which means the spinal cord actually protrudes from the body. We dealt with it, were dealing with all of it. We were ready for her to spend her life in a wheelchair, have learning issues, all of that, but she had an operation, not even a very serious one, and she just never woke up. Three months old, gone, just like that."

"I'm so sorry," John said. "I had no idea. That's just the worst thing ever."

"It gets worse," Beth said. "I told you I was working on my doctorate. While I was pregnant, I spent two months in Mexico City, working on Leguminosae research—bean research. Here's the thing—spina bifida is often the result of environmental factors, and Mexico City has the worst air pollution in this hemisphere. I might just as well have been chain-smoking Camel Straights. It's all my fault. My baby girl suffered and died, and all my fault."

"That is complete bullshit," John said.

Beth snapped her head around, startled.

"Really," John said, "Complete fucking bullshit. You know what killed Summer? The God of Shit Happens. Jesus, taking the blame for that…why not blame the lack of public transportation in the Greater Mexico City area, or blame the Spaniards for fucking up a perfectly good agrarian society by invading, or how about blaming the first peasant who wandered into the cone of an extinct volcano and said, 'This is a great place to live,' without considering that the topography was perfect for capturing stale, dirty air."

"But—"

"No, shut up. Because in addition to making yourself crazy with this egotistical guilt trip, you were planning on throwing your other three kids under the bus. You may not have noticed, but right now your kids only have one parent. It's a fucking miracle you aren't dead, or headed for a wheelchair or jail. You don't like shit in the air? Okay, let's get through this winter, because if your little stunt had succeeded and knocked out the power plant, you probably would have had another hundred thousand people on your tab, because that plant running right now is the only thing that's keeping them from freezing to death. Talk about a Crazy Eddie…" He subsided, just a head shake and a low growl before he turned and stared out the window to his left. "And what's worse, or funniest, or whatever you want to call it, is that the goddamn plant is running out of coal. I know guys who work here. About the middle of May, the stockpile is going to be gone and then…clean air and no lights."

"Listen," Beth said.

"I almost killed myself," John said, turning back to look Beth in the eye. "About a year and a half ago. Before the shit really hit the fan, but after I saw it all coming. I thought I was done, thought I'd done all I could to help prepare, and I just didn't have the heart to stick around and watch it all fall down."

"What happened?"

John shrugged, "Hell of a coincidence, really. The morning I'd planned to kill myself, we found out we were going to have a grandchild. I knew, or thought I knew, that Sarah's husband wasn't man enough to step up, to do what needed to be done." He looked back out the window and took another drink of coffee. "Hardest thing I've ever done, coming back to the world after I'd decided to step off." He shrugged and said, "But it had to be done. Doing what's right doesn't mean it *feels* right. Everything I'm involved with is just as big a pain in the ass as I thought it would be, and there isn't a day that I don't regret being part of it."

"John," Beth said, "I had no idea…"

"We're done talking about that," John said. "We're moving on. Look at that train over there."

"What?" Beth said, puzzled.

"Over there," John said, nodding to his left, "that train has been sitting there like three days, not moving, but there's exhaust coming out of the stack. What the hell would cause that? It's not unloading, not waiting for another train to pass, not shut down. That's a mystery."

"John, it's not your problem."

John started his pickup. "Everything is my problem. Let's go find out what's going on."

He casually turned the pickup into the ditch, engaged the four-wheel drive, and they bumped along through tall grass and small snowdrifts for nearly a mile until they reached the front of the train. Beth saw two heads peeking out the side window of the locomotive.

When John climbed out, walked around the front of the pickup, and leaned back against the fender, a door opened and a man in coveralls climbed down to talk to him. Beth rolled down her window so she could hear the conversation. She was a little nervous. She'd never been this close to a locomotive. It wasn't making much noise, but it was so enormous. It was like sitting next to a huge, slumbering dinosaur.

"Hey," John said.

The man just nodded.

"Are you okay? I noticed you've been sitting here for a while. This time of year, we don't really have that many tourists hanging out for days at a time."

"Bailey Yard," the man said.

"Yeah, that means nothing to me. Who's Bailey Yard?"

"Not a who, a what. It's the largest switching yard in the world, in North Platte, Nebraska. About half the trains in America go through it. Thousands of acres, two hundred tracks. It blew up last week. A train with chlorine gas and oil derailed. It wouldn't have been so bad except it was oil from North Dakota."

"So what?"

"What a lot of people don't know is that the oil from North Dakota is damn near as volatile as gasoline. A couple of cars of chlorine popped and that kept firefighters away from the fire."

John winced, filling in the blanks in his mind.

"While we were sitting here, we did the math—60 cars, 34,500 gallons per car. Two million gallons of oil burned. There's nothing left… it'd take years to fix it, and that's if anyone was fixing anything these days. We're sitting here because we don't know what else to do. We just want to go home. I've got a wife and three little kids. I haven't heard from them in two weeks."

"Where's home?"

"North of Phoenix, near Flagstaff. No way to get there from here, not by train, not now."

"Well…shit."

"Exactly."

John nodded toward the train. "What are you hauling here?"

"No end of shit, but nothing that is any use for getting us home."

"How many of you are there? Are you all headed the same place?"

"Yeah, but, so what?"

"Tell you what. You hang in here for a couple of hours and I'll try and figure something out."

"Why would you do that?"

"Because this train doesn't look like much to you, but to me it looks like Christmas Day. And since the railroad left you here, I'd be willing to take it off your hands in exchange for three tickets to Flagstaff."

"This train and what it's carrying is worth millions of dollars, mister."

"Yeah? What's it worth to you to get home? I'm offering you a ride home. What's the Union Pacific offering?" With that, John smiled, climbed back in the pickup, and, throwing an arm over the seat, backed the vehicle back to the closest road.

"Where are we going?" Beth asked.

"You ever play 'Let's Make a Deal'?" John asked. "Wipe the blood off your face and let's see what we can work out."

Their first stop was a car dealership in Milbank. The lot was cluttered with unsold cars, and there was only one person inside. He had a big belly almost obscuring a rodeo belt buckle. Blue jeans, a blue blazer, and a bolo tie completed his outfit.

"Hey, Jason," John said, "how the hell are you?"

"What do you want, John? Ten or fifteen new cars?"

"Yeah, what is this? Why so much inventory?"

"Corporate had them delivered, just to clear out their lots. Really. They shipped thousands, tens of thousands, all around the country. They sent me bills a few times and I'd tear them up. I haven't heard anything at all for a couple months. Who's going to buy a car? You can't get gas, and if you could, it would cost $20 a gallon, which no one could afford because no one's got work. I'm just here so I don't have to be at home. What the hell's going to happen, John?"

He glanced at Beth. She briefly wondered what he thought of her, but her nose was throbbing and her broken finger was sending sharp signals of its own. She was beyond caring what anyone thought of her and just wanted to get home.

John sat down in a customer chair and leaned back, teetering on the back legs. "I don't know, Jason. What I'm thinking is that we're on our own. That's why I'm here. I can't buy a car, but what I can do is get you something you can trade. And that'll mean your family is going to eat this winter. How's that sound?"

"It sounds like if it were anyone else talking, I'd be pretty damn skeptical. What do you have in mind?"

"I want that red one-ton pickup out there, the dual-fuel one with the full-size box. You're never going to sell it, we both know. It only gets about nine miles per gallon and it would cost, what, $60,000?"

"John, what do you have worth $60,000?"

"Such a deal I have for you. Right now, there is a train, 110 cars long, right outside of town. You give me that pickup and you can have any boxcar you want, to do with as you please."

"What's in them?"

"Not a clue. But you get to pick."

"It's not your train, John."

"Some people might think that. But here's the thing, Jason. Is anyone else offering you a boxcar of your very own? Look at you. You're sitting in a car dealership full of cars no one is going to buy. No one's said anything yet, but you're bankrupt. You've never done an honest day's work in your life and you have a wife and three kids who want to eat."

"So, what's keeping me from rounding up a few buddies and taking the whole train?"

John leaned forward and the front legs of the chair thumped to the floor. He leaned across the desk and said, "Nothing, Jason. There's nothing at all to keep you from doing that. Except, you're a good man, and that's in short supply in this world—and that's why I'm here talking to you."

"Ten boxcars."

"Deal. If you throw in floor mats and undercoating."

"Oh, fuck you."

◆　◆　◆

"Now what?" Beth asked.

John threw her the keys to the new pickup. "Follow me. We're going to the co-op."

At the co-op, they found another forlorn manager sitting alone in an empty store.

"What can I do for you, John?"

"I need one of those plastic tanks you've got piled up out there—five hundred gallons, fits in the back of a pickup—and then a few plumbing parts. All stuff you have too much of and will probably never need."

"How you going to pay for that, John?"

"Funny you should ask."

◆　◆　◆

"One more stop," John said. "The ethanol plant is still running, but that's just habit. I know a guy who works there and he says their storage tanks are just about full, and no one's coming to pick it up."

"Is this the way you ran things when you were a county commissioner?"

"Not really. This is kind of an acquired taste, like sauerkraut or escargot. It's easier if you're really hungry, and you have to be willing to throw up a few times."

♦ ♦ ♦

The winter sun was nearly set when they got back to the train, the watery light faint on the snow. The same overalled engineer climbed down from the locomotive.

"Here's the deal," John said. "That shiny red pickup is yours. Between the gas tank and what's in the bed, there's enough fuel in the tank to take you maybe 2,000 miles. Grab your stuff, climb in, and head for Flagstaff. Don't go through Denver or any big city, stay on the small roads and don't stop—don't stop for anything except to change drivers. I don't think anyone's going to be bothering you, at least not while you're moving and in the country. You'll be home in two days and then good luck to you."

"Why are you doing this?"

John shrugged. "Because I can. Because this is the best deal you're going to get, and because my people need whatever's on this train a lot more than you do. Because you work for a living and so do I, and that makes me want to trust you. And because we're both screwed by the people in charge and this, this is just a chance to do something that no one would see coming. And that's kind of fun, and fun's been in short supply."

The man stared at John for a brief moment and said, "You're crazy."

John gave a helpless shrug. "Buddy, you have no idea. But good luck to you. I'd suggest you smear some dust or something on this pickup, so it doesn't look new. If you stay in farm country, people will think you're a local and probably won't bother you. But seriously, don't stop, not for anything. Stay one mile under the speed limit, stay on small roads, and stay the hell away from any city."

He turned to Beth and said, "Merry Christmas. I got you a train. Let's go home. I need to tell Bobby what transpired today and you need to apologize to Oscar."

"Oh my God, Oscar. I don't really want to do that," Beth said. "I'm embarrassed."

"Yeah, well, kid, the 'want to' ship sailed a long time ago. From here on out, it's what we have to do that counts. Although, if Oscar gives you too much trouble, ask him what happened after the Marine Corps told him they didn't really need a one-armed gunny. Like that old saying, 'Sooner or later, everyone goes to the zoo.'"

"Is that really an old saying?"

"I don't know. If it isn't, it should be."

RACING DOWNSTREAM

"IT'S FEBRUARY," Alan said. "Feels like April."

"Weather can fool you," John said, "particularly in this part of the world."

They were sitting on the edge of the creek, watching water rushing downstream.

"Yeah, but ever remember the creek running this early?"

"How's your wife?" John asked, keeping his gaze firmly fixed on the tumbling stream. As always, he found Alan's presence vaguely irritating.

"She's fine."

"Really?"

"What do you want me to say, John? A month after her 60th birthday she got a diagnosis of early Alzheimer's. Now she's 68. On a good day, she knows me, and on a bad day, she needs a diaper. If our kids hadn't had to move home when things went south, I don't know what I'd have done."

"You didn't have to take care of her yourself, you know. She could have gone to a memory care unit years ago."

Alan said, "You know what wives and laxatives have in common? They both irritate the crap out of you." He shrugged, "When we got married, I said I'd take care of her. A deal's a deal."

"What do you want from me, Alan? You're in charge. Shouldn't you be off giving orders?"

Alan asked, "When's the last time you heard anything from outside the county? Phones have stopped working, internet, TV the same. New people have pretty much stopped trickling in, and the ones who do sound like they've left a nightmare. No news from St. Paul, and as to Washington… I don't even know if it's still there."

"Yeah, well… tough times."

Alan snorted, "That's what you call this?"

"Jesus, Alan, what do you want me to call it? The end of the world? I'm busting my hump trying to keep the wheels on the wagon, running as fast as I can to keep in one place."

"And you're doing a hell of a job. Truly, John, everyone thought you were crazier than a shithouse rat, and it turns out, you weren't."

"Alan… you sweet talker you."

"Okay, here's the deal. Two years ago, there were five thousand people in Big Stone County. Now there's twice that, maybe three times. Some of them have connections here—grandparents or cousins—but a lot of them are just people who headed west before Minneapolis caught fire. They stayed here because they ran out of gas or you gave them a meal. But what do we do now? We've got five cops, five, for the whole damn county. That's fine if it's five thousand people with half of them over 65, but it's not nearly enough to handle ten thousand strangers. Right now, they're just happy to be alive, warm, and fed, but people are assholes, John, people are assholes. Pretty soon they're going to want more."

The icy water churned and bubbled in front of them. In late summer, the creek had been dry; in early summer, it had been a trickle a foot wide; but now it was 50 feet wide and 10 feet deep, careening along through banks that had been eroded over hundreds of years.

"I love watching the creek," John said. "Remember when we were kids, we built a raft and were going to sail to New Orleans, till we hit the barbed wire on Johnson's pasture?"

Alan snorted, "Yeah, John, I remember that. I still have the scars. But I don't have time for another raft. There's a meeting this afternoon. Do you have any suggestions?"

John shrugged, "Two things. You could talk to Oscar. He knows everyone in the VFW and Ducks Unlimited—all the people who like to play with guns. He knows some of the more useful new people who've been working at the greenhouse. He can suggest who you should deputize. You should also talk to some preachers and social workers. I've often thought we had a flawed concept about law enforcement. We like to get people who are good with guns, but the guns only need to come out if you've failed at every other thing you've tried to do. You should find some people who are good at talking to people in distress. I don't think you need to worry about people coming from the north, south, or west. It's just the folks who trickle in from the Twin Cities who are going to be a bother. Put some roadblocks on 7, 12, and 28 and when someone shows up, give them the rules. If they won't agree, give them a ten-pound sack of cornmeal and turn them around. Anyone truly evil, like raping and murdering, shoot them behind the ear and tie them to a barbed wire fence on the county line with a sign nailed to their chest explaining what they did."

"Jesus, John!"

John shrugged. "Hey, you asked me…you don't need to follow my advice. I'd suggest you hang a sign on the bodies that says something like, 'In Big Stone County we obey the law and protect the helpless.' That'll start a sorting process right there. When you pick the guards at the roadblocks, you need to make damn sure that it isn't someone looking forward to shoving people around. If you do end up shooting someone in cold blood, and the person who did it doesn't throw up afterward, you better get them away from guard duty. You want more people here. You just want to be sure that they're not scared and looking to start a revolution. Second thing is, it seems to me that tired people with full bellies aren't going to be worrying about starting a revolution. You need to get people farming, making stuff, teaching stuff—get them too tired to whine. Most of them have families. Keep them safe and fed and busy, and most of your troubles go away. Jesus, Alan, look at what we need. We can get through a couple years, just living off what's on the shelves at a Walmart, but after that, how do we make clothes? How do we get medicine? Who's going to fix all the stuff that's going to start breaking? I know we can't make a microchip, but can we even make a generator? How the hell do you even make a spark plug? People are living on cornmeal, beans, and potatoes, but wouldn't you like a little variety? The people who look like they're going to be the most trouble? Put them in charge of making something. You love running things; I hate it. So…go run things. I've got more important things to do."

Alan stood up and looked at the tumbling water. "Hey, John," he said, "just as well we never made it to New Orleans. I don't think it's there anymore."

He stumbled through the melting snow back to his pickup and disappeared down the road in a cloud of gravel dust. John watched him go, and then his gaze was captured by the sight of a tall blonde figure picking her way toward his perch on the hillside.

"Jesus Christ," John muttered, "is it so hard for people to figure out that I'm out here alone because I want to be out here alone?" He turned back toward the creek, in time to see a chunk of snowbank tumble into the water and bob out of sight downstream.

He looked up when the faint chill of Beth's shadow covered him.

"Hey," he said, "how's your finger?"

She flexed it and said, "All better. Bruises went away, headaches are pretty much gone, and I hardly ever want to kill myself anymore."

Despite his mood, John laughed. "How are you and Oscar getting along?"

Beth plopped down in the snow next to him. "Better. He was a little cranky about wrecking his pickup, but it's running now, so there's that. That body shop guy from Minneapolis who's living in his duck-hunting shack thinks he can fix everything else, if he can take his time. I'm keeping him fed, so he's motivated."

"That's good," John said. "Oscar's had that pickup as long as I can remember. I don't even know if there's any original parts. I remember a juggler we saw once at the Renaissance Festival who was juggling a hatchet, a bowling ball, and…like a chainsaw or something. He talked the whole time, and once he said, 'This is the very hatchet that George Washington used to chop down the cherry tree. The head and the handle have been replaced, but it occupies the same space.' That's Oscar's pickup."

Beth nodded and stared at the rushing waters.

John said, "A lot of people laugh at that story."

"Sorry. John, I've got some news that you might not want to hear."

"Is there any other kind?"

"Here's the deal. All those varieties of beans you've been planting—they're adapted to the northern plains. Most of them won't pollinate if temperatures are above 64 at night. The past few years we've been pushing that, and it's getting warmer all the time, way faster than anyone thought. I mean, way faster. My colleagues and I used to think that we had until 2050 to breed heat-resistant beans, but that looks…optimistic. By a decade or two."

"So, what, this has all been for nothing? Everyone's just going to starve? We can build a greenhouse to grow vegetables in the winter; that's not a problem, but we can't cool off ten thousand acres of beans. How about all the other stuff we're growing?"

"Potatoes, same deal. The Incas had like 3,000 varieties of potatoes, so it's not like we can't adapt, but crop breeding takes time and the climate is changing so fast it's hard to keep up. Corn is a little muddy, because most all the corn here is a hybrid. Next year the yields are just going to fall off the table—you're going to go from 200 bushels an acre to about 20. We'll need to keep saving seed from the best plants for years and years before we get anywhere close to a useful yield. At best, it'll probably yield half what a corn plant does now. Wheat can take high temperatures, but it hates too much rain, and it's been raining a lot. Even the grass isn't adapted to what the climate is becoming."

"I can't believe you thought I wouldn't like to hear this." John stared at the snow beneath his feet, shaking his head back and forth like a trapped bear. "You know, when I was a commissioner, I always told people that if they were bringing me a problem they should also bring a possible solution. How you coming on that?"

"Do you know what a seed bank is?" Beth went on without waiting for an answer. "It's just what it sounds like—a whole bunch of seeds stored in a climate-controlled warehouse."

"Okay, where's the closest one?"

Beth took a deep breath. "The biggest one in the United States is in Denver. They have them in Chicago, New York, Tucson, Hawaii, Australia, India…" Her voice trailed off at the look John was giving her.

"Seriously, Beth, have you been listening to the news the past few months? How about have you noticed that we're not hearing any news anymore? Do you really think we could get to New York or Chicago? And if we could, do you think we could get into a seed bank without getting shot? And if the door were open, do you think we'd find anything useful? That's crazy." He looked for something to throw but had to settle for kicking a wad of slush downhill.

Beth took a deep breath. "No, John, that's not the crazy idea. *This* is the crazy idea. Have you ever heard of Svalbard, Norway?"

STILL CRAZY

"BOBBY, IS THIS YOUR STUPID IDEA?"

"No, John, I had no part of this at all. Didn't see it coming."

John was pacing back and forth in Bobby's shop. Like the rest of the buildings on his farm, the outside hadn't been touched in forty years, but inside was a machinist's dream, with tools and parts scattered all around. Bobby was sitting on a broken-armed chair in the corner, trying desperately to stay out of the way.

"I said, goddamm it, I said, when we started this crazy-ass project that anything that looked like it had been thought up in Hollywood was off the table, that we weren't going to do any crazy shit! And now you want to send a woman with three kids, a woman who's about an eighth bubble off level, to the fucking NORTH POLE! What the hell were you thinking?"

Bobby was amazed. In forty years, he'd never seen John much beyond irritated, and even that usually manifested as a wry grin and sarcasm. This was something very new, and even though alarming, it was fascinating to observe.

"John," Bobby said, his voice quiet and level, "This was not my idea. I don't know anything about beans or inadequate pollen transfer or any of that. What I do know is that this is a really smart scientist, and working in her chosen field of study, she's identified a significant problem *and* presented you with a possible solution. That's what I know."

John paused in front of a large cabinet-shaped device, with a monitor and a keyboard slung to one side.

"What the hell is this?" he asked.

"It's a 5-axis CNC machine," Bobby said. "It's a Hurco, with full Fanuc integration."

"What?" John shook his head in disbelief. "What can you make with it?"

"Well, anything. If you get the programming right, you just stick a piece of metal inside and it whacks off everything that doesn't look like what you want. Seriously—give me two tons of steel and I'll make you a '69 Chevy."

"Can you run it?"

"Sort of. I've gone through a shitload of the bits and other tooling learning. What's cool is that I can't order any of those, so I fix the old ones using a forge. So, 21st century technology with 10th century. Who knew?"

"Yeah," John said, "Who knew indeed. What did it cost?"

"I don't know. Hundred thousand dollars or so. I got it right before the shit hit the fan."

"How much money do you have, Bobby?"

"Probably none now. Do you want to get back on the subject?"

"Oh hell no, I don't want to get back on the subject, because it's a crazy subject. How are you going to get to the North Pole?"

"It's not the North Pole. It's like…800 miles from the North Pole. What we'll do is launch a boat in Lake Traverse, ride the Red River up to Lake Winnipeg, then take the James River to Churchill, and catch another boat for Svalbard. Easy peasy, lemon squeezie."

"When you were in school, did you read 'Canoeing with the Cree'?" John asked, "Eric Sevareid, he and a buddy took a canoe to Hudson Bay. Toughest thing he ever did, he wrote a book about it, talked about it the rest of his life, and that's the *easiest* part of your whole plan. And he did it *before* civilization collapsed. How about getting back, when you're paddling upstream instead of sailing downstream and carrying a ton of bean seeds? What the hell are you thinking?"

"EVERYONE'S GOING TO DIE, JOHN!" Bobby finally snapped. "You get that? Our seeds aren't going to work anymore. It's not my fault, not your fault, but there we are. There aren't enough walnuts and wild mushrooms in the county to keep everyone fed. We can't plant the whole place to grass and live off the buffalo. We need to farm, and to farm, we need crops that will grow. Fifteen thousand people right here, you've convinced all of them that you know your ass from your elbow. And how about all those other people all around us, who don't have a crop scientist telling them what's going to happen in a few years? Five years ago, I was out in Colorado, up in Wolf Creek Pass. Millions of dead trees, John, millions of them. The whole mountain was brown, and that was just because a little bug doesn't die in the winter anymore. Sure, new trees—different trees—will start growing, and that's fine if you're a mountain. It's damn hard to wait for Mother Nature to fill a niche when you've got a hungry kid to feed. If you have a better plan, fill me in. I'm dying to hear it." Bobby took a deep breath and went on, "It's the Nordic Seed Bank, John. They called it the Doomsday Vault—the place that would save the world if everything went south. Millions of seeds, hundreds of miles from the mainland. Norway should be better off than us—they have oil and refineries, grow most of their own food, get a lot of their electricity from hydropower, and have plenty of high ground. The warmer weather might actually be helping them. Plus, the seed vault is in permafrost, so let's say the place was looted—no one is going to steal a million varieties of seed. There's bound to be something there we can use, and because it's cold without refrigeration, they should still be viable. Getting there is going to be easier than getting to Chicago or Denver. That's just the truth."

John closed his eyes and rubbed his face hard. "Okay," he said, his voice muffled. "Dig out your National Geographic maps, and let's get a bunch of people around a table and talk about this. Okay?"

"Okay."

HELL, BUTCH

IT WAS A BIG TABLE. All the leaves were in it, even the crooked one that wasn't used except for Thanksgiving.

It needed to be big because the maps were big. Ancient National Geographics in three households had been scavenged to find the right combination of maps.

"Okay," Beth said, "It's a straight shot up the Red River to Lake Winnipeg, even if the river is so crooked it's about twice as far by river as by car. From there we have two choices: we can go to Norway House and up the Nelson River to Hudson Bay, or there's an actual road over to Thompson, which puts us on the Nelson River, too, except on a place where we're less likely to get lost. I don't know anything about Thompson."

Sarah said, "The newspapers call it the Crime Capitol of Canada."

It was the first thing she'd said, and five sets of eyes turned her way.

"I looked it up," she said, defensively. "It's a mining town. Thirteen thousand people the last time anyone checked, and it's got the highest rate of violent crime in Canada."

"Yeah," Oscar said, "but we're talking Canada. Their worst has to be like Des Moines on Christmas Day."

John looked like he'd bit into a lemon. "Let's just say you avoid Thompson. Doesn't do any good for there to be a road, because the road doesn't go all the way to Hudson Bay. How many dams are there on the river?"

"Six, at least," Beth said.

"So, you're going to have to take a canoe. There's nothing else that you can carry around a dam."

"I've been thinking about that," Bobby said. "What say we get a canoe, a big one, but we also get a boat with a good motor on it. Put all the gear in the canoe, fill the boat with as much ethanol as it will hold—maybe a hundred gallons—and then head north. Run day and night, twenty miles an hour. Two or three days should put you pretty well up in Lake Winnipeg. That would beat the crap out of the whole 'Canoeing with the Cree' scenario."

Oscar said, "Well, a boat burns about half a pound of fuel an hour per horsepower. So, at six and a half pounds per gallon, the range is going to be somewhere between 500 and 1,000 miles." He paused and shook his head. "Ethanol and boat motors don't really get along, so I'm guessing we'll run out of fuel about the same time we start breaking down due to water in the fuel. I agree about not shutting down, but if we go all night, I'd be worried about running into a log or a dead cow or something."

"People worry me more than logs," John said. "I'd want to go through Fargo in the dark, just putt-putting along trying not to be seen. Same thing with Winnipeg. We have no idea what's going on up there. If you need to stop, do it in a small town, a farming town, and trade them some of the bean seed that won't work for us, but should be just fine three hundred miles north."

Amy said, "Does anyone remember that there's an international border on the way? What if they won't let you into Canada?"

John said, "That's why Bobby's going along."

"What?" Bobby said.

John said, "Beth has to go. She's the only one who knows what seeds to get—which ones are useful or valuable. Oscar should go because he never does anything stupid. He's like a stupid antibiotic.

And Bobby needs to go in case there's a need to talk someone into *doing* something stupid. That's his best thing." His face made a motion that might have been a smile. "Trust me, I know."

Sarah shrugged, "Daddy, when you're right, you're right."

Beth said, "John, I can't go. I have children."

John said, "I know you have children, Beth. Whether you have children or not isn't the question. The question is, do you want to have grandchildren?"

In the silence that followed, Oscar said, "So, the plan is to send a woman, a cripple, and a bum—no offense…"

"None taken."

"…in a canoe, to save the world, and if we need help, we'll get it by selling magic beans."

"Well…yes."

"Okay then. Sounds like a plan."

"How are we going to get home?" Bobby asked. "Because that's important, right?"

Oscar said, "Oh hell, Butch, the fall will probably kill you." He looked around the silent room and said, "I'm not going to explain it. You got it or you didn't."

TOO TIRED TO CRY

ABBY WOULDN'T STOP CRYING.

Beth stared helplessly. She'd stopped crying herself, but that was just due to exhaustion.

"Momma, you can't leave us," Abby said. "Daddy isn't here and Sam and Danny fight all the time and we're not home and you JUST CAN'T LEAVE!"

"I don't want to, sweetheart," Beth said, for what felt like the hundredth time. "It's my job, I have to go do some work."

"We're your job, Mommy, we're your job. Tell someone else to do it."

"I can't," Beth said, "I just can't. No one else can do it, and in order to keep you guys safe, someone has to. It's kind of like grocery shopping—I have to go get the seeds for us to plant to grow food. I just have to. Sarah will be here, and Amy, and I know you like John. They'll all take care of you until I get back."

"How long will you be gone?"

"I don't know, baby. It's going to be a while."

"Then go," Abbby said. "Just go. And I don't care if you ever come back." She stormed out of the room. Beth heard her footsteps going upstairs and couldn't miss hearing the bedroom door slam.

Turns out she wasn't too exhausted to cry after all.

APRIL FOOL

"HOW MUCH OF YOUR FREIGHT TRAIN IS LEFT?" Bobby asked.

"Shit, I don't know. I'm having a little trouble moving the tanks of sulfuric acid. Where's a serial killer when you need him? Where the hell were 12 tank cars of sulfuric acid going? I do know we had to trade 5,000 board feet of 2 x 12's for a 20-foot canoe."

"That's not so bad."

"Yeah, well, do you want to know what the paddles cost?"

Bobby laughed. "Come on, that's funny and you know it." He slid another book into a plastic sleeve and maneuvered the package into an electric sealer. A brief stench of melting plastic and he added the waterproof package to a large pile at his elbow.

"What are you working on now?" John asked.

Bobby's dining room was hot and cluttered. He'd finally caved in to necessity and had a half-dozen people staying with him, all bachelors with relaxed standards in housekeeping. The house smelled better than when it had just been Bobby and a tomcat, but not by much.

"I have two complete sets of The Foxfire Books. Back in the '70s, this schoolteacher in Appalachia sent his students out to interview old people in their neighborhood about the old days—how to butcher a hog, build a log cabin, all that stuff. They made a whole series of books that people stopped caring about when the Internet was invented. Now that you can't Google, people are going to have to learn to read again. I think I'll peddle them one at a time." He looked around. "I've already sealed up the blacksmithing guides and the ones on working wood without power tools. As a marketing tool, I'm thinking I'll package hop seeds with the book on brewing beer."

"That's great. I'm glad you're working on your marketing skills."

Bobby paused, staring down at the stack of books. "You know, I wouldn't tell this to just anyone, John, but I'm fucking terrified."

"It's Canada and Norway," John said, tipping his chair back against the wall. "Nothing bad happens there. You should know that; you read books. All those spy books take place in Jamaica or Casablanca or Constantinople. Those are the only places people get hurt."

"You're a big comfort, John. Do you even realize Constantinople has been Istanbul since, like, 1930?" Bobby still didn't look up, and John was surprised to see that his hands were trembling.

"C'mon, man. What's the worst that could happen?" John shrugged, acknowledging the absurdity of the statement. "I know this is dangerous, but everyone dies, Bobby. I don't think it will be much safer here."

"You think I'm scared of dying? Jesus, John, I haven't cared about living or dying this century. I'm scared of fucking this up. The only things in my life I've done right are make money and drink." He picked up another book and sealed it in its plastic envelope. "Why am I going on this little venture instead of you? You're the responsible, boring one."

"You think I haven't thought of that? You don't think I'd rather be fighting rabid beavers in Manitoba than dealing with what's going to happen around here this spring? I don't know how many people made it through the winter. My guess it'll mainly be back-to-nature types who had a basement full of canned applesauce and some guys with guns who barricaded themselves inside a Walmart. Most of them are probably going to hit the road this spring looking for something better, and some of them are going to end up here. You know our sheriff—do you want him to handle that on his own?"

What could only be described as a giggle made its way past Bobby's lips.

"You're going instead of me because I've hardly ever even been out of Minnesota. You and Oscar and Beth have been all over the world. The three of you have traveled more than the rest of the county put together. Plus, someone comes running to me asking for advice about every six minutes—all of a sudden I'm the indispensable man. Plus, the three of you have the skills. What the hell would I add to this expedition? You think I wouldn't rather be paddling through an empty wilderness than dealing with everything here?" John's chair thumped back to all four legs. He got up and walked around the room, disturbing random piles of literature. He looked up and said, "We're both screwed, Bobby. You're going to get eaten by a polar bear on Hudson Bay and I'm going to die of scurvy or a ruptured appendix. We just can't tell anyone that's how the story is apt to turn out. We've got to keep pretending we know what we're talking about."

Bobby didn't meet his gaze. "Okay then," he said, "What's your opinion on The Anarchist's Cookbook? Do Canadians want to learn how to make bombs out of hydrogen peroxide?"

"I would say it depends on the marketing. Take it along. You can always throw it at a polar bear. What's it say about sulfuric acid? We have plenty of that."

"Yeah, well, I don't think we have time to package up a bunch of acid. I'm just about done packing up the books. Beth has all her seeds in bags, and Oscar has his armory stored and he's figured out how to hold a canoe paddle with only one hand. We're leaving tomorrow."

"Any special reason?"

"First of April, April Fool's Day. Can you think of a better time to start?"

"Seems…appropriate."

Bobby picked up another book, slid it into a plastic sleeve, and arranged it carefully in the sealer. An electric buzz and then the stench of melting plastic wafted through the air. John sat down and carefully leaned back in the chair until his head hit the wall. They didn't talk, and the only sound to disturb the silence was the intermittent electric buzz.

DROPPED OFF

"WHERE YOU DROPPING US?"

All four of them were crammed uncomfortably in the cab of John's pickup, heading north with a little Lund boat on a trailer behind them, with a twenty-foot Mackenzie Kevlar canoe perched on top of it.

"Just north of the White Rock dam on the Bois De Sioux. That gets you a good start. It doesn't sound like we can drive as far as Breckenridge. Folks say things have kind of gone to hell up there. Here's hoping no one is watching the river. It's not like the Mississippi—except in the spring it hardly flows, so it's not really the center of the community. Hell, I can't even remember if I've ever seen a boat on it."

There were nearly to the Traverse County line and Beth saw a police car with its flashers on waiting for them. As they approached, it pulled in front of them and led the way. She nodded toward it. "Is this really necessary?"

"Don't know," John said, "They're a little closer to Fargo and they've had some problems we haven't had. I talked to their sheriff—he didn't mind using the gas to give us an escort because their gas is already starting to go bad—another six months and it'll only be good for lighting campfires. Then it's diesel until it runs out, then…horses."

"Wow," Beth said.

"Yeah," John said, "things go to hell faster than you'd think. It's nothing new—the Jews in Warsaw, the Tutsi in Rwanda, they could all tell us stories. We're just lucky that so far we aren't dealing with genocide—just stupidity."

"Speaking of things going to hell…" Oscar said, digging into his travel bag and bringing out two small revolvers. He handed them to Bobby and Beth.

"Ruger LCR 9mm revolver. Most common ammunition in the world and it's double action. All you need to do is pull the trigger and it'll go bang."

Beth inhaled deeply and blew it out in a long, exasperated exhale. She held the weapon and turned it around in the midday light. It was tiny, black, and ominous looking.

"How do I aim it?" she asked.

"Beth, if you need to use this, there will be no aiming involved. You pull it out of the holster, shove it against the stomach of the guy you're going to shoot, and pull the trigger five times."

"That was a little more graphic than I needed."

"No, it wasn't. This isn't about aiming—this is about being willing. You need to wrap your head around the idea that we are apt to meet someone who doesn't care if your kids ever see you again, and you need to be able to picture him standing between you and your children's future. Then you have to be willing to take his life and let his blood run down your arm and drip off your fingers. That's where your head has to be at, from now until we're back home again."

"Jesus, Oscar," Bobby said.

"Hey," Oscar said sharply, "you two convinced me we needed to do this, that the future of everyone we care about is in the balance. Okay, fine, we're going to do it. But this was my job, okay? This is what I did. If we land in some shit, I want all the late-night/beer-and-tequila philosophical discussions on the sanctity of life out of the way ahead of time. Here's what we got: I sawed the barrels off an old double-barrel shotgun. That thing is practically as easy to use as those revolvers, although it kicks like a son of a bitch. It's mean and it looks mean. Then I have my old Remington 700 with the big scope. If we're around people, I'll sit up high, holding that thing. Anyone who knows guns will know I can drop them at about a mile away if I want. I'm thinking that's our stupid deterrent. Plus, it's the tool for deer, caribou, or anything we might run across that looks edible. So that's my plan, and that's what I think you all need to internalize. Beth, what do you think? Keep in mind, if you ever need to use that revolver, it probably means I'm already dead. So, as a personal favor, considering you wrecked my pickup, if I get killed, I want you to be able to kill the son of a bitch that did it."

She looked up, peering through the dirty windshield at something no one else could see, then turned flat blue eyes toward Oscar and said, "Five times. Got it. You'll have to show me how to reload. But then we'll be square on the pickup, right?"

"Here we are," John said. The deputy helped get the boats in the water and the motor started with the first pull. Goodbyes were short, and John didn't wait for them to get out of sight before he climbed back into the pickup and headed for home. He left the boat trailer at the landing.

Maybe someone else could find a use for it.

RIVER NORTH

THE RIVER HAD SUBSIDED from its spring flood, but it was still flowing fast, brown, and cold. The banks were high and made out of brown clay. It was impossible to see anything beyond them, and the river curved enough so you couldn't see more than a half mile in front or behind. Oscar sat in the prow, big rifle in his hands, alert and intent. Bobby sat with his hand on the tiller, leaning slightly to the side for a clear view forward. The big canoe bobbed in their wake, twenty feet behind at the end of a rope.

Beth faced backward and shouted over the engine, "This is feeling less stupid to me. I thought we'd be sitting ducks in the middle of a big river, but you can't see anything, can you?"

Bobby shook his head. "Not many houses next to the river because it floods so often, and when it's not flooding, it's not all that appealing. Plus, there just aren't many people here. I think we'll only have to really worry when we go through towns."

"It's so dirty!"

Bobby shrugged, "We're in the middle of the Red River Valley. It's basically the bottom of a mud puddle—topsoil fifty to a hundred feet deep and dropping off just a couple inches to the mile between here and Lake Winnipeg. You throw a cup of water on the ground and it'll wash some dirt away. It's pretty clean—now that we've had a couple of years without fertilizer or herbicides draining into it. You could probably drink it, if you could strain the mud out."

Beth opened mouth to say something, but the strain of shouting over the boat motor made it seem like too much bother. The April sun didn't have much power, and the occasional splashes over the side of the boat were shockingly cold. She hunkered down in her coat and leaned back against one of the barrels of ethanol. It wasn't a pillow, but it gave a little. She put her hands deep into her coat pockets and closed her eyes. The boat motor, the slap of water against the hull, and the gentle sway as Bobby negotiated the curves of the river blended into white noise, and she sagged into a restless sleep.

The engine throttling down is what woke her up. Her neck hurt, and she had a moment where she was baffled as to where she was, then it all came back to her.

She sat up in the boat and saw Bobby standing up in a half crouch. He noticed she was awake and said, "Beth, go up there by Oscar and make sure we aren't going to hit anything. We're just coming into Breckinridge. I have no idea what we're going to find."

Beth nodded and worked her way to the front of the boat. Oscar looked down at her and nodded, "Up there, on the right. The Otter-tail River joins up, and then this turns into the Red River of the North. A little bigger and a little more current." He was speaking above the gentle pounding of waves against the hull and the muted throb of the outboard motor. "We haven't had anyone from this direction come to Big Stone County for most of the winter."

"What does that mean?" Beth asked.

Oscar shrugged. "I have no idea. None, zero, zip. In a normal year, there would be millions of bushels of grain stored here. No one should be starving, if you can live on cornmeal, whole wheat bread, and whatever the hell you can make from soybeans. But people might have gotten damn cold, and cold can mean dead pretty easy in this part of the world. Or maybe the whole town moved into the high school and they're keeping it warm from body heat, and they're all living on corn bread and waiting for some suckers to try and sneak by in a boat so they can resort to cannibalism without eating someone they went to elementary school with."

"So, what should I do?" Beth asked.

"I don't know. Try to look friendly, intimidating, and, you know…tasteless."

"What do you think about shutting down the engine and just drifting for a while? Maybe we'll hear something. Maybe no one will hear us."

"Shit, I don't know," Oscar said. "It's not a bad idea." He turned toward Bobby and pulled a finger across his throat. Bobby nodded and cut the engine.

Initially, the silence was profound, but as their ears adjusted, small sounds crept in—various waterfowl, the hissing of water against the riverbank. The boat slowed and the big canoe overtook them, bumped twice against the stern, then settled back to the end of the rope when Bobby gave it a push.

"Nothing," Oscar said. "Jesus, there's 10 to 12 thousand people living here. I don't hear a damn thing." His voice was pitched low, barely carrying the length of the boat. As they slid around a bend in the river, captives of the current, a faint waft of wood smoke came their way. A big house loomed over the riverbank and what looked like a candle gleamed in the window. A minute later, the river curved again and the house was lost behind them, no indication of how it or its people were faring. The darkness was deep and the silence profound.

A large splash startled them all, but it was just a section of clay riverbank collapsing into the stream.

"If it's all the same to you," Bobby said, "I'd just as soon start the engine and get the hell out of here. This is freaking me out."

Oscar looked at Beth and Beth shrugged. "Yeah," Oscar said, "let's get the hell out of here." The little outboard popped to life and the boat picked up speed. "So," Oscar said, "we're about an hour and a half into this little venture and I'm already freaking out. I can tell this is going to be fun."

"Dark when we get to Fargo?" Beth asked.

"That's the plan. I'm not saying it's a great idea, or even a good idea, but it's what we're going with."

♦　♦　♦

Beth was a little sick to her stomach. The river looped and twisted, turning back on itself and only slowly making its way north. The weak April sun was setting, and the shadows reached nearly across the river.

The further north they went, the wider the river became and the more convoluted. The current was picking up, too, as various small tributaries added their water to the mix. The river marked the border between Minnesota and North Dakota, with Fargo to the west and Moorhead to the east. The bed of the river was thirty feet below street level, with parkland and trees marking the boundary.

Bobby shut off the boat motor, and silence descended on them once again. It was pitch dark and quiet all around them.

"Shouldn't we be seeing something?" Beth asked.

"No skyscrapers here—the tallest buildings are like 10 to 15 stories high. But you're right—we should be seeing something. Why is it so dark? We have electricity, why don't they?" Oscar asked.

"Well, we have a power plant five miles away, and a smaller percentage of crazy people who want to blow shit up," Bobby said. Beth was glad for the darkness. She seldom blushed, but when she did, her pale cheeks were a blossom of embarrassment.

A shimmer of light flickered on the horizon. "Looks like a fire," Beth said, "a big one."

They swept around another corner, and the light grew brighter. Soon they could hear voices, loud and angry.

"Jesus Christ," Bobby said, "I want to go home. This is not fun. I've had fun, and it was nothing like this."

"Shut up, Bobby, and stay ready," Oscar said. "We may need to leave in a hurry. We've got no options here. We have to take this river north, and whatever is in the dark up there will be worse in the light."

They rounded a curve in the river and gaped in amazement at the scene in front of them.

"What the fuck?" Oscar said.

Bobby giggled. "Of course," he said, "I should have seen that coming. What's next, space cowboys?"

Beth said nothing, and her mouth hung open. In front of her, several large fires dispersed the darkness. A crowd of people shifted, ebbed, and flowed, shouting orders at each other. Halfway down the bank was a huge wooden form that looked exactly like a Viking ship. It loomed out of the darkness like a figure from an ancient dream, the dragon's prow reaching for the water and the tall mast swaying high above.

"Relax," Bobby said, "It's the Hjemkomst."

"It's a VIKING SHIP!" Beth said, "What the hell?"

"Yes, Beth, it is—it is a Viking ship," Bobby said. "Back in the '70s, a teacher sawed up a bunch of oak trees and built it in a potato warehouse. I don't know why…winters are long up here. I suppose it makes as much sense as a bowling league. He died of cancer, and his kids sailed it to Norway and then shipped it back here and built a museum around it. So, yes, it is a Viking ship, and those are wannabe Vikings in front of us. I think that means we need to focus."

Someone in the crowd noticed their silent approach and pointed and shouted. Soon the whole crowd had turned their attention to them, and one waded out in the river and held up his hand. Oscar pretended it was just a friendly wave and waved back, but another half dozen men splashed into the river and grabbed the prow of the boat.

"Who the hell are you?" the leader said. He was dressed in Carhartt coveralls and waders, and he had an old .45 in a shoulder holster. His beard was black and wild, and his hair cascaded from underneath an NDSU stocking cap. The dim firelight did nothing to show his features—Oscar could see nothing but a gleam of eyes.

"Nobody special," Oscar said. He heard a faint splash to his left but kept his attention on the man in front of him. "We're just passing through, gonna meet some friends in Winnipeg. What are you doing here? Looks like you're going boating."

"Yeah, well, there's nothing here, nothing anywhere. No power, no food, no nothing. The power went out a couple months ago. The grocery stores were almost empty before that. Two weeks ago, the natural gas stopped. Just stopped, man. I don't know if somebody blew up the pipeline or the people in charge just stopped caring. Whatever, doesn't really matter. Everyone old is pretty much dead, anyone who had somewhere to go took off long ago. A bunch of us were going to break into the Armory—it's full of guns and ammo, maybe even tanks and rockets. Then we'd be in charge, but we'd just broken in the front door and some asshole blew it up. It just blew, burned for days with ammo and shit cooking off." He shook his head at the memory and then motioned back to the Hjemkomst. "We're gonna sail this baby to Norway, just like they did when they built it. It's going to be reverse pillaging—it'll be great."

"I thought they left from Duluth?" Oscar asked.

The man waved airily. "Whatever. We're going up to Hudson Bay and leave from there."

Oscar opened his mouth, thinking of the six huge dams on the James River, and then closed it again. It was going to take a long time to get the fifty-year-old Viking ship into the water and under sail by a bunch of people who had no idea what they were doing. If he explained that it was a bad idea in the first place, they might just want to take the boat that was already floating.

"You know," the man said, "your rig looks like it could be handy. How about if we let you join us?"

"Thanks," Bobby said, "you've got a great ship there. Good luck with it, but we're really just going to keep plugging away by ourselves."

"I'm not sure that's one of your options," the man said, and reached for his .45.

Oscar felt a bump under his feet and then Beth surged out of the water and stuck her revolver in the man's ear. He realized the splash he'd heard must have been her going into the water on the far side of the boat and the bump was her swimming underneath.

"Oscar," she said, "you told me I got to kill the next one." She leaned close and whispered, "I have to say, the end of the world makes me miss a decent haircut and good tequila, but you know what makes up for it? Being able to kill people and no one can do a thing about it. Is that cool or what?" She kissed him softly on the cheek and said, "I can pull this trigger five times and you'll go from a six-foot-tall pirate to five-foot-tall corpse, just like that." She slipped her free hand inside his coveralls and said, "Tickle, tickle, tickle."

Oscar brought his sawed-off shotgun up from his side. "Bethie, hold off a second." He turned away from the leader and aimed the shotgun at the men holding the boat. "Here's the deal. In ten seconds, you're going to be dead, and so are about half of your friends." He spoke loudly enough to be heard on the riverbank. "I can't promise them, but you for sure." He paused for a moment and then said, "No, change that. I think I can get most of them. Once in Afghanistan I dropped six Taliban in three seconds. Of course, I was armed a little differently, which helped. On the other hand, it's been my experience that it's not so much what you're packing, it's if you're willing or not. And I've always been willing." He let his gaze fall on the men holding the boat. "You guys aren't ready. You all have both hands where I can see them. You have to let go, grab for something that goes bang, and wonder if you have a round in the chamber. Me, though, I have to move my finger a quarter of an inch and people start to die. Who thinks that gives me the edge?"

Just a shadow of the First Marine Division crept into his voice. "Even with needing to reload, I'm confident I can get a bunch of you." He stopped to let that sink in and then dialed it back to his quiet, reasonable voice. "If you like my canoe so much, just bounce on over to Cabela's, and I bet they have a dozen or more sitting around. Who's going to steal a canoe in the middle of winter? We're not in your way, we haven't taken anything of yours. In the end, I'm sure you can take what we have, but it will cost more than you're willing to pay. If you're willing to let us go, I'm willing to try and talk Bethie out of killing you." He raised his voice. "If this guy's your leader, you need to understand that he's going to be dead soon. I'd suggest you get back to work getting that ship in the water because in a week the water is going to drop far enough so that thing won't float, and then you've got nothing." He thumbed off the safety. The metallic click carried across the water, and everyone holding the boat lifted their hands and took a step back. As the boat began to float downstream, Bobby started the engine with one hand and pulled Beth on board with the other. Oscar kept the group under his shotgun until they reached a bend in the river and the fire faded into the darkness behind them. No one said a word for five minutes, then Beth's teeth could be heard chattering over the sound of the boat motor.

"C-c-can you guys see me?" Beth asked.

"Can't see a thing," Bobby said.

"Good. I'm going to change clothes because I'm freezing."

"Go ahead," Oscar said, "I won't peek. Really." Bobby snorted. "I think you're safe, Beth. We're both pretty much scared of you now."

They heard wet clothes slop against the bottom of the boat, then the zipper on a bag.

"Hey, Beth," Oscar said, "where did that 'tickle, tickle, tickle' come from? Because that was freakin' terrifying."

"I don't know," Beth said, "I just kind of…went with the crazy."

"That's fine," Bobby said, "Kudos, seriously. And hang onto that in case we meet any other counterfeit Vikings, but you're going to keep that under wraps around us, right? The whole…crazy."

"Maybe. Oh shit, I opened the wrong bag. Bobbie, can I borrow some clothes?"

"Anything you want, Beth. Seriously. Anything."

Beth giggled. After a moment, the other two joined in. The giggles died away, then Beth said, "Bethie?" and it started them back up again.

They motored north in the darkness, and behind them, Fargo burned.

AT THE BORDER

"ARE WE CLOSE TO THE BORDER?"

"I don't know," Oscar said, "We've been twisting and turning so much, for all I know we're back in Big Stone County."

"Seriously, though, we're close, right?" Beth asked.

"I think so. We just have to keep following the current until someone tells us to stop."

The river was brown and fast, twice as wide as it was in Fargo. Scrub trees lined the banks. They hadn't seen a house for an hour or more.

"Flat land, no rocks, no bedrock," Bobbie had explained. "The river could cut a new channel at any time, and if your house is close to the bank for the scenery, the river could go through your backyard, front yard, or living room just like that."

"Don't complain," Oscar said. "It's making our life easier. It's like the river is invisible to people. No one seems to be watching." A moment later he said, "Here we go. This must be Pembina." They motored slowly through the heart of a small town, although the high banks kept them from seeing much of it. "Heads up now—the border is only going to be a mile or so away."

In a couple of minutes, they came around a corner and saw two men in uniform lounging on the riverbank. They looked startled, then waved the boat over. Bobby steered to the bank, and Oscar jumped ashore, holding an anchor. He plopped it down in the mud and swore gently as Bobby cut the engine. The boat pivoted around the anchor rope, and the canoe floated by, then turned back as its tether brought it up short. For a moment, the silence was profound.

"This is an international border," the guy in the Canadian Border Services uniform said. "You can't just zoom on through. Actually, we're not really letting anyone through right now."

Bobby nodded. "Okay, I understand. Do you have a boss I could talk to?"

"You bet," the man said. "You stay right here. I'll go get him, because this is something he's probably going to want to see." He clambered up the riverbank and disappeared.

"What's your plan?" Oscar asked.

"I think I'm going to tell him the truth," Bobby said.

Beth laughed out loud. "Let me stretch out. This could take a while. Mind if I take notes?"

"No," Bobby said. "It's going to be great. Canadians are wonderful people. Am I right?" He directed his question toward the other man, who was wearing an American Border Patrol uniform.

"I dunno," the man said, "sometimes they can be assholes. This should be fun." He paused and said, "For me, anyway."

In a few minutes, two men slid down the bank, and one of them, a little older and with a jaundiced eye, said, "Well?"

Bobby took a deep breath and said, "Okay, here's the deal…"

He finished up ten minutes later, after giving what Beth felt was a reasonably complete and relatively truthful account of their plans.

"That's the dumbest goddamn thing I've ever heard," was the response.

Bobby shook his head. "I can't argue there. But here's the deal. In normal times—say, five years ago—if we came along here, you would search out boats, look at our ID, make us sign a couple documents, and then you'd turn us loose and laugh yourselves silly after we were out of sight."

"No, we probably wouldn't have waited that long."

"Anyway," Bobby went on gamely, "we're not asking that much. We're not actually asking for anything out of the ordinary. And we're willing to pay for passage."

The man bristled. "These are hard times," he said. "Strange times. And no one knows what's going to happen next. But it could be a pretty significant mistake to try and bribe us."

"No, no, no," Bobby said. "I'm not talking about bribery, not talking about giving you anything. But as you said, these are hard times, strange times. We brought along some stuff that we don't need, that we have too much of, but could really be of value to the people living around here. What we have is something for your community, something to make life just a little easier." He took a deep breath. "Tell me, does anyone here like beer and chili?"

Fifteen minutes later, they were back on their way, having left behind a third of their bean seed and half of their hops, along with two books on home brewing and one on blacksmithing.

"That went well," Beth said. She was huddled in the bottom of the boat, trying to stay out of the way of the occasional splash over the gunwales.

"Thanks," Bobby said. "I knew that if I could just get him talking…"

"All we have to do now," Beth interrupted, "is get through a major city, a huge lake, a few hundred miles of wilderness, and once we reach Hudson Bay, we'll know the easy part is over." She squirmed over and rested her head on a bag of millet. "You should probably save some of your words. I'm going to take a nap."

"Yeah, well," Bobby sputtered,, "pretty bold talk considering you're still wearing my clothes!"

"I appreciate the loan, Bobby, I really do," Beth said without opening her eyes, "if only they weren't a little tight in the shoulders and loose in the waist."

Oscar kept his attention on the river, alert for logs or other debris, but after a moment, his shoulders started to shake.

◆　◆　◆

"Bobby, look," Oscar said.

He pointed forward at two boys fishing in the river. They were dressed in dark clothes with heavy work shoes and hats that in another life Beth would have described as fedoras.

"What do you think?" Bobby asked.

"Could work," Oscar said.

"What are we talking about, guys?" asked Beth.

"Those boys," Oscar said. "They look like Hutterites."

"What are Hutterites?"

"Like Amish, except they use modern equipment and they all live together—like eat their meals in a dining hall, stuff like that. There are a couple colonies at home. Good people, good farmers. People don't like them because they're tough competition, but their word is usually good—sharp businessmen, but not crooked and not mean. If those boys are from a colony, they might be just who we want to talk to." He guided the boats toward shore and slowed to a stop. The boys pulled their lines out of the water and watched, warily, silently.

"Hey, guys," Bobby said, "I'm Bobby; this is Beth and Oscar. We're here from Big Stone County. Are there any grownups around we could talk to?"

One of the boys was slightly taller. "I'm Sam Hofer; this is Levi."

"Hey," Oscar said, "I know some Hofers."

"Are they okay?" Levi asked. "We haven't heard from the Big Stone Colony in months."

"They're fine," Oscar said, "I just bought some chickens from them. They're doing well—it's just hard to stay in contact."

Levi said, "Sam, go get Amos and them." Sam clambered up the muddy bank and disappeared from sight.

"So," Levi said, "Why are you here?"

Bobby opened his mouth, closed it again, looked at Oscar and Beth, and then said, "You know, Levi, it's a long story. Can we wait until everyone gets here?"

An hour later, Beth looked around in amazement. The dining hall was huge, with room for a hundred or more. When they were escorted in, the children were just finishing and tables were reset for the adults of the colony. The food was terrific—Beth could see a huge commercial kitchen and gleaming equipment whenever the double doors opened.

After a short prayer, people dug in, with the firm appetites of people who worked for a living. There was little conversation until the first helpings of chicken, mashed potatoes, and sweet corn disappeared.

Beth couldn't keep from glancing around. A woman about her own age seated across from her laughed and said, "You seem curious. Would you like a tour?"

"Honestly, I'd love one," Beth said. "I just didn't know how to ask without being rude."

"I'm Sarah Stahl," the woman said. "Let's go for a walk. Keeps me from doing dishes."

Sarah was about Beth's height, attractive, with dark hair and eyes. She was wearing a long dress made of fabric printed with small flowers. She had on sneakers and a dark cap over her pulled-back hair.

Beyond the double doors of the kitchen was another room just for baking, adjacent to a massive pantry lined with glass jars of canned vegetables and a walk-in freezer.

"Do you want to see the butcher shop and smokehouse?" Sarah asked. "I don't like the smell so much."

"Let's see the gardens," Beth said, "I'm more of a garden gal."

"Me too," Sarah said, "I've always loved plants."

There were what looked like two football fields planted just with potatoes. Rows and rows of onions, carrots, and cabbages stretched out, with orchards on the north and west sides, performing double duty as both windbreak and food production.

Beth thought of what they'd seen in the past three hundred miles, and how, even though it seemed bad, the worst of it was far from here—and so much worse she could hardly fathom it.

"This seems like paradise," she said.

"Oh, I don't know," Sarah said, "there are men here."

It was so unexpected, coming from someone dressed as if she were from a century in the past, that Beth laughed out loud.

Sarah laughed as well and blushed just a little. "Now, you don't need to tell the men," she said.

She went on, "These are strange times, and pardon me for saying, you're a strange group to be traveling through. You must have a reason."

Beth told her.

"Oh my," Sarah said, "and you seem like a serious person. Is the situation really that bad?"

"I think so," Beth said. "It's what I've been studying most of my adult life. The climate has been changing for quite a while, and the pace is accelerating beyond most worst-case scenarios. There's something called thermohaline circulation…"

"Like the Gulf Stream," Sarah said.

"Very good," Beth said.

"Beth, we may wear bonnets, but we do go to school," Sarah said.

It was Beth's turn to blush. "Sorry," she said, "I'm just not used to most people understanding what's going on. The bottom line is that what most scientists thought was going to take a century is going to take about a decade, because there is so much cold, fresh water entering the ocean that these giant currents appear to be shutting down. Plants adapt to changing conditions, but they don't adapt that fast. We need those seeds, as many different kinds as possible, and frankly I'm not sure we've got a real plan for getting them. We were lucky to get through Fargo and luckier yet that the border guards were in a good mood. And the easy part of the trip is over."

"You've convinced me," Sarah said. "We've been worried about the weather for years. Some things are growing better, but not all of them, and that's a worry. You say this looks like paradise, but you should understand, we have nearly 10,000 acres, and most of it will go unplanted because we don't have the fuel, seed, or chemicals to do the job. We're back to subsistence living, and if it weren't for the solar panels and windmill, we'd be much worse off. We're only an hour from Winnipeg and we don't go there anymore—we have food to sell, but no one there has anything worth having in trade, so for now we're just trying to take care of ourselves and our neighbors."

"Okay then," Beth said, "good to know."

"I'm not the one you need to convince," Sarah said. "You'll have to run this past the Zullbrueder—it's like the colony council. It's just men—I won't have a vote."

"Any tips?"

"Maybe."

An hour later, Beth was back in the dining hall, but this time there was just Bobby, Oscar, and a dozen men in dark clothes, hats, and heavy beards.

A troop of young people had brought their belongings from the boats, and the gear was in an untidy pile in the corner of the room.

"What do you want from us?" Samuel Glanzer asked. He had a full gray beard, and his hat was pushed back, revealing a high, pale forehead. "Let's say we believe you and we agree with you. I don't see what we can do to help you." His English was clear and fluent, but with a guttural undertone that indicated it wasn't his first language.

Bobby said, "Well, before we figure out what you can do, I'd like you to understand that we're not beggars. We think we can make it worth your while. We think leaving friends behind us as we leave will help us when we're on our way back." He turned to Beth and nodded.

She gestured toward their packs and said, "We have ten different varieties of edible beans there that should grow in your climate as it changes. There are some other garden seeds, and an assortment of books that you might not have in your library. What we're offering you is, literally, priceless. And one more thing…" Beth reached into the pack at her feet. "Mr. Glanzer, I took a walk around your farm. It's lovely, and I especially admired your trees. Shelter from the storms, building material for an uncertain future. It takes people of vision, people with a hope for the future and a commitment to coming generations to plant trees. I know roughly where the other Hutterite colonies are in Manitoba, and a couple of them are on our proposed route. What do you think you, your relatives, your colleagues would place as a value on these?" She brought out several pine cones, each one as large as her hand. "These are from giant redwoods. They haven't grown in this part of the world for hundreds of thousands of years. But each cone has about 250 seeds and about half of them will germinate. Sprout them in your greenhouse, and by the time they're ready to plant, the climate will be ready, too." She leaned forward, her blue eyes capturing the attention of everyone at the table. "Think about it. In *your* lifetime, these trees will be fifty feet tall. Your children will see them rise to over a hundred feet, and your grandchildren…" She leaned back, but left the cones on the table. "Think of the legacy. Think of the usefulness. Think of the message you're giving your descendants of the confidence you have in them. You've kept the faith for over 250 years. Imagine how this place can look in another 250 years. I want you to help us because it's in your best interests, and it should be profitable for you as well. These cones, though…they're just a gift, whether you help us or not, because I just like the idea of a redwood forest on the shores of Lake Winnipeg."

Samuel looked around the table and then said, "We'll talk. There's an empty house you can stay in tonight—get showers and wash clothes. Tomorrow morning, after we break fast, we'll talk again."

On their way through the door, Oscar turned to Bobby and said, "I thought you were supposed to be the silver-tongued devil. After that little stunt at the Viking ship and what just happened, makes me wonder why either one of us came along."

Bobby shrugged. "Too late now. But I'm not saying you're wrong."

NORTH

SPRING HAD FOLLOWED THEM NORTH.

At Samuel's suggestion, they hadn't emptied their packs at his colony. Even though the colonies stayed in contact with a shortwave radio, they were all freestanding communities, so spreading out the seeds and books between everyone who helped on the trip made for a far more seamless voyage.

The first leg had taken them from south of Winnipeg a hundred and twenty miles north to near Gimli, on the west side of Lake Winnipeg. They made the trip in the cab of a semi converted to run on canola oil, with their canoe in the trailer riding cushioned on 800 bushels of soybeans. Their driver was an exuberant twenty-year-old named Aaron, dressed in black clothes, a snappy fedora, and an ambitious black beard. They were in the oldest truck owned by colony, a 2004 Peterbilt, and Aaron explained why.

"You need a truck made before 2007—they changed engine design then around low-sulfur diesel, which was a good thing for emissions, but it makes them not work well with biodiesel. Doesn't matter so much, because as soon as this engine breaks down we're back to walking anyway, because the parts chains are broken—nothing is coming out of China anymore or anywhere east of the Mississippi River. Toronto, all up and down the Great Lakes…it's a big mess from what we've heard. Almost everything that could break on this thing is something that needs to be made in a factory—lots of computer chips and special alloys that we don't have access to."

"You seem pretty cheerful about it." Beth was sitting next to him while Oscar and Bobby stretched out in the sleeper of the big cab. She was used to the faint accent the Hutterites all had. Their fluency in three languages, their cleverness and community, and their ability to dip into the large world and fish out what they needed and throw back what they didn't was a little intimidating.

Aaron shrugged, "The first diesel engine was built in the 1800s and it ran on peanut oil. I figure I'm as smart as any 19th-century German—if they made it, so can I. The solar panels that give us electricity in the colony are going to last 30–40 years. By then, we'll have figured out something new, something we can make ourselves."

"Seriously?"

"Seriously. We use the outside world, but we don't need it. Look at Hutterites, Amish, Mennonites, all those groups that are self-contained and a little suspicious of all that's new. Those are the people to watch. If no one messes with them, they'll figure out how to cope. Big cities—that ship has sailed. I feel bad for the people who know nothing else, but I think they're all going to die if they don't leave, if they aren't dead already. You can't be independent in a city, can't depend on yourself. People were hungry three days after trucks stopped delivering food in the city. By now, it's just rats prowling around a dump." He smiled at Beth, a twenty-year-old's shit-eating grin.

Beth didn't smile back. "Damn, I'm sorry I talked to you today."

Aaron shrugged, "It's not my fault. I don't tell anyone where or how to live."

Bobby sat up and swung his legs over the edge of the bed. "How close are we to Gimli? We might want to check it out."

"Why?" Beth asked.

"Well, in Norse mythology, Gimli is the name of the paradise where the survivors of Ragnarok go to live. We sure wouldn't want to take the chance that is *the* Gimli."

Aaron and Beth locked eyes.

Beth said, "Bobby, you know more shit that doesn't matter than anyone I know."

Bobby nodded, "Yeah, I get that a lot. You have to admit, skipping Gimli could be a big mistake."

"Let's chance it," Oscar said, "Even if it is paradise, it's a Norwegian paradise. That might not be a big enough upgrade to make it worth the trip."

Aaron laughed, "You guys are funny. We were talking, we're going to miss you."

Bobby said, "Well, we'll try to stop in on our way back and give you some more laughs."

Aaron laughed louder, "That's not going to happen. You guys are going to die. No way you get to Norway and back." He shrugged, "It's a pity though. You're funny guys."

A week later, a cherubic 80-year-old with a fringe beard and a strong accent helped them pull their canoe out of the back of an ancient blue pickup.

"End of the road," he said, "We're close to Grand Rapids. Next stop for you will be Norway House." He pointed northwest into Lake Winnipeg. "If you went straight across the lake, it'd be about a hundred miles, but that'd be stupid—paddling nonstop, it'd take you four or five days, and that's if the weather was in your favor, which it won't be. Stick close to shore and it'll take you a week or so if things go well. Don't get eaten by a bear or by mosquitoes and try not to be trampled by a moose. Otherwise, it'll be great."

"Thanks for everything," Bobby said, "I don't know what we would have done without you."

"Yeah, me either. And don't think that doesn't weigh on my conscience. But on the off chance, the miracle chance, that you make it, bring back some good stuff. We're going to need it."

The air off the big lake was still cold, even though the ice was long gone. They slid the canoe into the water and spent a long time loading it. At their last stop, they'd been gifted 50 pounds of beef jerky, courtesy of a cow that had broken its leg and was removed from the gene pool. With four hundred miles of paddling ahead of them, the consensus was that it was going to take them at least a month, traveling through wilderness with an occasional outbreak of civilization.

When the pile of supplies on the bank was distributed into the bottom of the canoe, with scant room for three passengers, the travelers paused and locked eyes.

"Well," Oscar said, "saddle up. It's going to be great—no more damn strangers disturbing the silence."

"Good attitude," Beth said, "but, you know, stupid."

It was almost noon, but with a favorable wind, they made nearly twenty miles before camping for the night.

It was a good beginning.

THE LONELY LAND

THEY'D DECIDED EARLY ON TO AVOID PEOPLE as much as possible.

"There's only like 5,000 people spread out over the next 400 miles," Bobby said, "We don't have much, but it might look like a lot to some of them."

"I don't know," Oscar said, "Have you ever eaten beef jerky for a month?"

"I think I'm with Bobby," Beth said. "When the shit hit Winnipeg, people could have gone three directions toward the best places to raise food in the world. Do we really want to cross paths with ones who decided instead that they wanted to go hang out in a hostile, trackless wilderness?"

It seemed like a solid plan, but now Beth was cold.

Cold, wet, hungry, and terrified.

Over the years, she'd spent a lot of time in canoes, but it had always been a sunny-day, small-river experience.

The Nelson River was huge, and it was in the midst of its spring flood. In many places, the banks were hard to discern, with water flowing five feet deep through the pine trees along the edge. They were making incredible time, captured by the current and flying toward Hudson Bay. Every day's progress was purchased at the cost of gritted-teeth concentration from the time they shoved off in the morning until they beat their way to a camping site before dark.

Their first big portage, around the dam at Jenpeg, had actually gone pretty well. They'd heard the roar of water going over the dam at about the same time as a small airport showed up on their left. They pulled off to the side and, without even unloading the canoe, carried it a quarter mile to a small bay downstream of the dam. A man fishing had pointed without speaking when asked where the main channel of the river was. They were on Cross Lake and headed north in a matter of minutes.

Whenever they'd exited a lake and gotten back on the river, the current had been like a hungry animal. They'd laminated the maps of their route, splitting them up into twenty-mile segments. It had all seemed obvious, but the reality of traveling through a wilderness was completely different, with trips down several dead-end alleys costing them days of travel.

They'd portaged around the dam at Kelsey and were headed out into Split Lake. The current spit them into the lake, and Bobby, in the front of the canoe, pointed toward a wooded island a mile from shore. He and Oscar dug their paddles into the water and Beth steered the canoe toward the rocky shore.

It had only taken about a week for them to settle into a camp routine. Beth set up the tent, Bobby scrounged for firewood, and Oscar would head to the water's edge with a fishing pole.

"Tonight," he said, "I'm thinking lake trout. How about a buck-tail jig next to that downed log over there?"

"Just, I dunno, food. Please," Bobby said, "I can't tell the difference anyway."

"Dude, are you sure you're from Minnesota? I'm ashamed of you."

"I don't play hockey either. Deal with it, and catch some supper, or it's trail mix and tea."

Beth tuned them out. She had grown fonder of both of them throughout the trip, but they were both such…guys sometimes. She had no idea what male imperative was met by the constant bantering, but there must be some reason.

She found a small clearing under some young pines. After checking for rocks and pine cones, she set up the tent. Moss and pine needles softened the granite, and there was room for a small fire under the woods, where it couldn't be seen from the shore. It was the best campsite they'd had in a while. There had been a few nights camped on a greasy clay riverbank and a few more on bare rock ledges. The immensity of the land had in turn shrunken all three of them, so now they were unconsciously inconspicuous, like mice creeping around the edge of a room. She walked away from the campsite and threw a rope over a branch twenty feet in the air. Before bed, they'd stuff anything that smelled like food into a canvas bag and pull it up into the tree. Oscar always slept by the door of the tent, although if a bear were to seek them out in the dark, there was no real guarantee it would come through the door.

She heard a whoop from Oscar and cheered up a bit as she interpreted the sounds to mean there was fresh fish for supper.

By the time the massive lake trout was cleaned and cooked and a couple cups of tea were drunk, along with a handful of raisins for dessert, the sun was setting. Beth set out some oatmeal to soak overnight and then wormed her way into her sleeping bag, leaving her boots inside the tent but off her feet. After the first rainy night, they'd started bringing all their gear inside the tent, too. It left them just barely enough room to turn over in the night but avoided morning sogginess, which they all agreed was worse.

"Another day," Oscar said, "easy peasy lemon squeezy."

"Plenty of time for things to go to hell," Bobby said.

They didn't say the same thing every night, but almost.

Beth said, "Guys, I've got something to say."

There was a brief silence, and then Bobby said, "Okay?"

"I just want... I'm just glad that this whole trip, both of you haven't made this... awkward. Me being a woman and we're jammed together all the time. This could have been awful for me, and you've both been really respectful. I appreciate it a great deal."

"That's it?" Bobby asked. "That's the big reveal?"

"Pretty much," Beth said.

"You are married," Oscar said. "Us country folk have a strong belief in the sanctity of marriage."

"There's that," Bobby said, "and there are a few other reasons you probably didn't need to worry. Remember that night in Fargo when you dived under the boat and tickled that guy you were threatening to kill?"

"Pretty clearly, yeah."

"Well," Bobbie said, "I've been pretty much terrified of you ever since. Another entry in the ledger is that you smell really, really bad. And, speaking for the team as a whole and not just for myself, Oscar is gay, which pretty much takes you off the table for him as well."

"Oscar's gay! When did that happen?" Beth felt her cheeks flame in the darkness. "Oh shit, that sounded dumb."

"A little bit," Oscar said, "but to answer your question, I believe the current theory is that I've been gay my whole life."

"Nobody told me!"

"There is a chance," Oscar said, "that those of us who knew might consider it none of your business."

"Those of us who knew? Who knows?"

"Well," Oscar said, "now that you mention it, I guess everyone but you.

"Okay," Beth said, "I'm traveling through a wilderness cheek and jowl with a gay man whose advances I've been planning how to gently reject and another guy who sees me as a repulsive psychopath. That's not awkward at all."

Oscar said, "Good talk."

"Plus, you know," Bobby said, "you snore a little."

"Shut up," Beth said.

"REALLY good talk," Oscar said.

The night was silent except for the lapping of waves on the rock ledge, a mild breeze through pine branches.

And a few snores.

♦ ♦ ♦

"How long has it been since we saw a human being?" Beth asked.

She was in the center of the canoe, leaning back against a pack. They'd almost stopped paddling, just staying alert for floating debris or the occasional violent rapids that hadn't been tamed by the dams.

"Maybe a week, or a little longer," Oscar said.

"Where do you suppose everybody is?"

"Look around, Beth," Bobby said, gesturing at the riverbanks. "It's scrubby trees and peat bogs. Nothing to do here except catch fish and dodge mosquitoes and polar bears."

Over the last hundred miles, the forest had diminished in height and density. It was almost impossible to stray off of solid rock without sinking into the spongy tundra. Beth knew that there was a road off to the left, leading to the last dam on the river at Sundance, but it had been days since they'd heard any traffic at all.

"The thing is," she said, "at least these people must have electricity. We know what the dams are producing isn't going anywhere."

"*That* was something to see," Bobby said. "I'd like to know the story behind that."

"Not me," Oscar said. "I'm perfectly comfortable leaving that a mystery."

It was before they got on the river, not so very far north of Winnipeg. The road was following the massive transmission lines coming from the northern dams, and they'd paused by a scene of massive devastation—toppled high lines, crumpled steel towers, and masses of tangled wires. It went on for miles until they came to the cause: a massive D9 Cat, burned black, with a broken electrical line wrapped across the hood and a scorched corpse still sitting behind the controls.

"I think we were right the first time," Bobby said. "The First Nations people didn't like it when they started building dams, and they never got over it. That bulldozer was just some payback."

"But the dams are still there—tearing down the transmissions lines didn't fix anything!"

"How you going to tear down a dam, unless you have about twenty tons of dynamite?"

Oscar said, "You may be overthinking. First, you do what you can, not what you want to. Second, people do dumb stuff—that may have started with something as simple as a case of Molson and some keys left in the Cat. Third, despite rumors to the contrary, there are some assholes living in Canada."

"But that guy, whoever he was, killed so many people. Those lines kept the lights on for millions of people, and it was winter…" Her voice trailed off. The river was nearly silent, and there was little noise of any kind disturbing the soft spring sunlight.

All three of them were on edge. The river had defined their lives for so long, but that journey was coming to an end, along with all certainty of what was going to come next. They were physically uncomfortable as well. Oscar and Bobby had long since passed endearing scruffiness on route to dangerous vagrant. Beth had gotten her period a week ago, which had led her to some pointless private fretting about whether it was sharks or bears that were attracted to the scent of menstruation. Their food wasn't running short, at least not in terms of quantity, but they'd long since exhausted variety. Worn down by the concentration needed to stay afloat on a dangerous river and worried about the horizon of an uncertain future, the long conversations they'd used to have now trailed off into silence. They spent the long daylight hours navigating river hazards, and the nights trying to relax tight muscles and frazzled nerves.

A faint rumble in the distance made Bobby cock his head.

"That should be the dam at Sundance," he said. "Last one. Did we decide what we were going to do?"

The previous two dams they'd slipped past in the dark, out of an excess of caution or a simple reluctance to explain themselves once again. One dam had been dark and quiet, the second had yellow light streaming from the windows and soft music reaching through the darkness. They'd left them both behind, but this was going to be their last opportunity to get a heads-up as to what was facing them once they reached Hudson Bay.

"I think we have to stop," Beth said. "Anything they tell us will be more than we know now."

"I guess I'm with you," Bobby said.

"I'm not saying you're wrong," Oscar said, "but we better be ready. I mean…really ready. We are at the end of the road in almost every way possible."

They came around a bend in the river and saw a small dock sticking out into the slack of the river. They pulled in, unloaded the canoe, and Oscar slung it up on his shoulders after putting on one of the packs. Beth and Bobby each slung packs and filled their hands with the rest of their bags. Together, the trio lumbered down the path toward the small cluster of buildings around the dam.

A dog started to bark as they approached. A figure appeared in a window, and then a door opened and six men came out.

"Wow," the first one said, "where the hell did you come from?"

"Down the river," Bobby said, "headed to Churchill."

"What the hell for?"

"That's probably a longer story than you'd want to listen to."

Five of the men were dressed in company coveralls. The sixth had on faded camo, and an old 30-30 dangled from one hand. Oscar's world narrowed down to him and nothing else. There was a vibe coming off him that reawakened instincts he'd been damping down for years. The man was tall and lean, with a cleanly shaved face and neatly trimmed hair. He smiled at Beth and said, "Shoot, we've got nothing but time. Let's go inside and chat awhile."

Oscar said, "We really don't have much time. Thanks for the offer, though. Any news from further downstream?"

Bobby and Beth exchanged startled glances. They'd spent half a day discussing a plan, and now Oscar had abandoned it in the first 30 seconds.

"C'mon," the tall man said, "I insist. Do you have any idea how long it's been since we've had a beautiful woman stop by? We'll have a drink, you can clean up, do some laundry, get a hot meal…"

"No," Oscar said.

"And I said, we insist."

Oscar smiled. "Geez, let's not get off on the wrong foot." He swung the canoe down off his shoulders, pulling the sawed-off shotgun from under the front seat as he did, and shot the man twice, once in the chest and again in the face.

The other five men hit the ground almost as fast as the corpse.

"What the fuck, Oscar," said Bobby. His mouth hung open and his eyes were wide.

In the aftermath, the screams of a flock of ravens filled the ringing silence.

"Okay," Oscar said, "here's the deal. I don't like a man holding a gun and saying things like, 'I insist.' That's just a note of clarification for all of you." He broke open the 12-gauge and popped in two fresh shells. "I also don't like people disturbing my balance with creepy smiles and insinuating comments to my travel companion." He didn't point the shotgun directly at the men, but he didn't point it away, either. "Keeping that in mind, tell me about your dead friend."

"He wasn't our friend," one of the men said, his face plastered in the gravel of the parking lot. "He showed up here a couple weeks ago, said he was on a hunting and fishing trip and just kept coming north 'cause there was nothing left behind him." The man was almost babbling. "He didn't say nothin' about nothin'—he was keeping us fed with his fishing and otherwise just sat and played cards with us. We haven't seen anyone else in weeks, maybe months."

There was a long pause, and then Oscar said, "Okay. Let's start over, with the ground rule that if I feel you are threatening any one of us, you'll all die."

No one moved. Oscar continued, "I'll go first. Hi, guys, it's nice to see friendly faces. We've come by boat from Minnesota, headed for Churchill. If you want to share some of our rice, beans, and last night's fish, we'd really like to pick your brains about what's a little further downstream."

No one moved until Beth went over, knelt between two of the men, and said, "It'll be okay. We're not going to hurt you. That guy started down a bad road and he had no idea what was waiting for him. You do, now, so everything will be alright. Seriously, we don't want any trouble and we might even be able to help you out a little. C'mon. Let's go inside."

"Go ahead and take the deer rifle," Oscar said. "No sense in letting it get rusty out here. That blood will wipe right off." He smiled, but it wasn't a particularly nice smile. "Trust me, I know."

One of the men slowly picked up the rifle, and everyone went through the door and inside the building. The dog stopped barking, and in the parking lot, the blood slowly seeped away into the gravel. After a while, the ravens quieted down as well.

◆　◆　◆

Two of the men were named Dan, and Beth concentrated so hard on that, she never did keep the other three straight.

She bustled around the kitchen in the dormitory building. They had rice, beans, and fish of their own, but their spice cabinet was

211

largely untapped, and there was a largely unused 50-pound bag of flour.

I'm guessing none of them know how to bake bread, she thought. Her first task was to set out several loaves to raise overnight. After that, she started a batch of brownies.

She tried to keep her back to the men talking around the big round table. She'd never seen herself as the little woman in the kitchen while the men settled business in the other room. Today, though, she welcomed the time alone. Since the world had crumbled, she'd seen more bodies than she cared to remember, but to this point, no one who'd died simply because she was in front of him. She was still shaking a little and working hard at not making eye contact with Oscar. She heard the mumble of voices but managed to tune out the actual words.

An ancient bulb of garlic she'd found in the back of the refrigerator was helping her recreate an old New Orleans rice and beans recipe when she heard Oscar's voice.

"Hey," he said.

"Hey yourself," she replied.

"Is there anything we need to talk about?" he asked.

"What the hell, Oscar," she said without turning to face him. "You killed that guy. Are you sure that was the right thing to do?"

"No," Oscar said, "but it doesn't matter now."

"What! What do you mean it doesn't matter now?"

"Hey, I can't undead him. It's over, and from here we deal with the ramifications."

"But why… I've heard lots of guys say worse things, worse things in front of you, and nothing. Why now?"

There was a pause of several seconds, and then Oscar said, "You know, many years ago there was a psychology experiment in a college. They gave twenty bucks to a bunch of different students and told them to buy posters to put up on their walls. With half of them, that's all they did, but the other half, the kids had to list the reasons why they were picking a particular poster. They checked back a year later and most of the students who'd just seen a poster and said, 'Oh, I like that one,' still had them up on their walls. The kids who'd been made to justify their purchase, most of them had long since chucked their posters. We're in the same place here. I just shot him without thinking about it too much, and if I'd spent more time thinking through it, I might not have. And then Bobby and I might be dead and you might have spent the night getting raped. Or not."

Beth turned around, and when Oscar met her eyes, he gave a rueful shrug. "But since you asked, here's what I think triggered me. First of all, it was like Sesame Street—'one of these things is not like the other.' These guys here are clearly working stiffs—engineers, welders, or the like. The guy I shot didn't look like he belonged : wearing different clothes, a different haircut, standing a little behind and to one side of the rest of them. His eyes locked on you right away, which you can't blame him for, 'cause you're a good-looking woman, but he didn't even pretend not to. To me, he looked like the guy at a buffet staring at the prime rib station—he knew what he wanted and he didn't care who knew it. I've seen that look before, in places where the rules have gone away. He was going to shove his way to the front of the line. He had a…sense of ownership, that he was top dog, that he was in control. That's not good in a church meeting, let alone in the wilderness when he's holding a gun."

"Yeah, but he was, was holding a gun."

"So what? Guns don't bother me. Truthfully, Beth, the man is dead because I was cold and tired. When I took the canoe off my shoulders, I could have knocked him over with it and stood on his head until we got things sorted out. I could have talked some more until I was sure what his deal was, could have done a lot of things. That was just more bother than I was willing to go through at the moment. Instead, he's dead, I'm not, we're warm and clean, and you're making what smells like the best meal I'll have had in a month. Everybody dies, Beth. I feel a little bad about killing that guy, but not too bad. That's who I am, that's what I do. I've done it a lot."

"I haven't."

"Yeah, well, that's okay. You did fine in Fargo when the chips were on the table. I'm not suggesting you get used to this. I hope you don't, I hope you don't need to. And, you know, don't scorch the rice."

"Dammit!"

Over dinner, one of the Dans did most of the talking. "We've got ten turbines here," he said, "and we're just idling along with one of them, just keeping our lights on. The road is usually closed in the winter—they run crews back and forth by helicopter. When things got dicey, they sent us unmarried guys here, and after the lines went down, no one came at all. We don't know what the hell we're going to do."

"I don't know," Bobby said, "if I were you, I might hunker down here as long as you can. If you've got family on a farm and you've got enough gas to drive there, that would be your best bet. But I'd wait until summertime before I made the try. You're warm here, got some food…if the fish are biting, I don't think I would hurry away."

"I still have some seeds—lettuce and the like. You could set up a greenhouse and balance your diet a little. You don't have to worry about leaving the lights on—you've got all the power in the world."

Bobby asked, "So, not to be a baby, but what about polar bears?"

The other Dan shrugged, "They're just starting to come off the ice. I don't think you'll run into any, but the problem is, if you do, they're probably going to be hungry bears."

"Fantastic," Bobby said.

"What's your plan when you hit Hudson Bay? It's a long way to Churchill, and that's a big body of water."

"Yeah, you know," Beth said, "we didn't really expect to make it this far. Let's not muddy the waters with excessive planning now."

"Atta girl," Bobby said, "welcome to the Dark Side."

"Shut up. Eat a brownie."

◆　◆　◆

They stayed one more day, cleaning and drying their gear. When Beth got up the first morning, her eye went to where the body had been, but it was gone. Oscar saw her glance.

"Don't fret," he said, "I went out last night and buried him over in the edge of the woods. Made a little marker, just in case someone shows up looking for him."

"Why did you do that?"

Oscar looked puzzled. "Who else?"

"Who else indeed."

Early on the second day, they left. Dan and Dan and the other three waved goodbye, although they weren't sorry to see Oscar go. They'd never stopped looking at him as if he were a grizzly bear inside a cage with a broken lock.

"Saddle up," Bobby said, "Big water awaits! Cold, salty, polar bear-infested big water!"

"I don't know which is the bigger tragedy," Beth said, "that I'm on this trip, or that we brought Bobby along."

"Tough call," Oscar said. "But remember, it's too late to change one of those factors, but not the other. Little boat, rough water…accidents can happen."

"Hey!" Bobby said.

They launched the canoe in the slack water away from the spillway. In a few minutes the dam disappeared behind them, leaving behind five men, three fresh loaves of bread, and one corpse.

It was a long day, but at the end of it were the waters of Hudson Bay.

"What's the plan?" Oscar asked.

"Take a left, paddle like hell, and try not to drown or get et," Bobby said. "The maps show a manmade island right in the mouth of the harbor. Nobody lives there or anywhere close to there. I figure we spend the night and see what tomorrow brings."A few minutes later, Beth said, "Is that it?" In the distance was a wrecked ship on a tiny island, with a beat-up old bridge connecting it to the mainland. There was a smattering of trees and nothing else. There were no signs of any recent human habitation, and not much signs of life of any kind.

"You got it," Bobby said. "Port Nelson. Furthest north ghost town in Canada."

The trees provided enough firewood for a real campfire, and after dark, they sat on the edge of the island, the fire at their back and Hudson Bay in front of them. They'd spent a month trying to be invisible, with tiny fires stamped out at dusk, but from here on out, they needed to attract attention.

The wind had calmed, and there was little sound but the lapping of waves at their feet and the distant cries of a multitude of birds.

"We shouldn't be here," Beth said.

"Little late for that," Bobby said. "I kind of think we're committed."

"No, that's not what I meant," Beth said. "I know we have to be here. We…shouldn't have to be here. None of this was a surprise. Everyone knew the climate was changing, everyone knew our grid was too vulnerable, everyone knew we leaned too hard on fossil fuels and *everyone* knew our politics were broken and nobody was fixing any of it. I'd say I'm angry, but it's more than that. I'm just so damn sad about all that's lost, and that makes me angrier."

"You know," Bobby said, "I take a lot of shit from—well, from everyone—because I happen to have a brain that latches onto random shit. Usually, it's a waste, and I know that, but every now and then, I'm actually of some use, and this is one of those times." He took a drink of the hot water, which was now their only beverage. He looked without favor at the metal cup and said, "Jesus God, what I wouldn't give for a beer, or a cup of decent coffee or…almost anything." He took another drink and said, "About a decade ago, I saw an article about the roots of various words. I've forgotten all of them, except this one. The word 'anger' is derived from a Scandinavian word, 'angry,' and the accurate meaning of that word is 'grief at the wrongness in the world.' The point is, what makes you angriest is when there is just something so wrong in the world, and what you're really feeling is sadness that you can't make it right. That's what you're feeling now, Beth. Grief at the wrongness in the world. I can't change that, but it's probably good for you to know."

"I like that," Oscar said, "I really do. 'Grief at the wrongness in the world.' I've seen so damn much wrongness, if tomorrow things go south, it'll be okay with me, because unlike the guys in ties, I'm doing what I can while I can."

"Fine with me, you go right ahead," Bobby said. "I want to live forever. If a polar bear comes, you're the one getting whacked."

"Good to know," Beth said. "I'm going to bed. Easy part's over."

"Easy part's over," Oscar said.

Bobby said, "Yeah. The easy part is over."

BIG WATER

IN THE MORNING, a hard wind from the north stirred up mammoth waves, along with a smattering of cold rain that kept them in the tent all day.

The next morning dawned clear and still, and they were in the boat and moving shortly after daylight.

A vast expanse of water was to their right and a long sandy beach was to their left. Beyond the beach was tundra, lakes, and in the distance, a dark pine forest.

Slow-rolling waves made the canoe pitch and toss, but they made good time to the north.

"There are a couple of things we need to keep in mind," Bobby said. "Wapusk Park is one of the best polar bear birthing areas in the world. It's a little early for that, but it's something we might want to keep in mind. Second, in the past decade or so, grizzly bears have started moving into the area as well, making this one of the few places in the world where polar bears and grizzly bears share a range."

"What, no killer whales or tsetse flies?"

"Well, there's beluga whales—not as cool a name and probably won't eat us—and it's a little early for mosquitoes. Sorry to disappoint you."

"How long before Churchill?"

"Several days, if things go well."

"Got it. Keep paddling."

"What the hell is that?" Oscar and Beth spoke simultaneously.

"What are we talking about?" Bobby said, swiveling his head.

"Is that an island?" Beth asked.

"What?" Oscar said. "There's no island. I'm looking at the shore up there. Is that thing alive?"

"Oh shit, oh shit, oh shit, oh shit," Bobby said. "It's a polar bear. It's definitely a bear."

"Out to sea," Beth said. "Maybe it won't see us."

"Won't see us," Oscar said, "but the breeze is right toward it. It's going to smell us."

They bent over their paddles, digging deep into the salty water and heading away from shore.

Oscar spared a glance backward. "Son of a bitch, it's in the water, heading this way."

"Maybe it'll get tired," Beth said. "How far will a bear swim?"

"The record is 220 miles," Bobby said. "Of course, that was over nine days. Maybe we got a lazy bear. How long can you paddle without stopping?"

Beth didn't answer, but dug deeper.

For long minutes there was no sound except their gasping effort.

Oscar looked back again. "We're gaining on it," he said, "but it's still coming on."

They didn't talk again. They were headed into the swell and it was enough to make progress a shuddering, jolting, odyssey.

Beth was gasping, "We're miles offshore. If the wind comes up, we're screwed. We won't even be able to turn toward shore without tipping, and that's if the bear gives up."

"Not giving up," Oscar said. "It's gaining now."

"Rifle," Bobby gasped. "Shotgun?"

"Closer," Oscar said. "A lot closer. Keep paddling."

"Heading for the island," Beth said. "Maybe it'll be calmer there, easier to shoot."

Over the panting, a strange buzzing noise filled the air. For a moment no one looked up—too tired, too focused to care. Oscar was the first to glance up, seeking the source of the noise.

"What the fuck," he said. "It's a drone. It's a goddamn drone. Where did that come from?"

The other two looked up. The drone was painted a light gray, blending in with the spring skies, and it was clearly looking at them. It was hovering 50 feet in the air, and its camera lens was pointed directly at them.

"Bear first," Oscar said . "Paddle harder. I'll get the shotgun."

Beth and Bobby dug deeper, their shoulders trembling and burning with pain.

The drone left, swooping out of sight in a matter of seconds. Now they could hear the bear, coming closer with only two people to paddle the massive canoe. It was breathing through its nose, a snorting blast every few seconds. Oscar had the shotgun out and was fumbling for slugs instead of buckshot, his crippled hand slowing the process.

Another noise, familiar but unexpected, burst into their consciousness.

"It's a HELICOPTER," Bobby said. "What the hell?"

"Beth," Oscar said, "I don't think that's an island."

The helicopter was over them in a matter of seconds. A rope with a net on the end came down toward the canoe.

"MH60," Oscar said. "It's a Navy copter. I think they're offering us a ride."

"Take it," Beth said. "Grab that net."

Bobby grabbed and clambered up into the net. Beth followed, pulling two of their packs with her. Oscar was last. He started to hand the shotgun up to Bobby, but saw a figure in the door of the helicopter holding a compact black rifle. He pointed at the shotgun and shook his head. Oscar nodded and dropped it back into the canoe. He grabbed with one hand and got his foot in the webbing. They were reeled up. Beth and Bobby were helped into the helicopter. Oscar looked down in time to see the polar bear grab the edge of the canoe and tip it over, spilling all their supplies into the water. The bear tore open the bag with their food, and the last thing Oscar saw was a loaf of bread disappearing in two bites, followed by a hefty serving of smoked fish.

The helicopter was hugely noisy, and when the outside door was shut, it was barely any quieter. Beth could see two pilots in the front, and there were two other crewmen in the back with them.

"I'll be go to hell," Oscar shouted, pointing. Beth and Bobby swiveled around to see what he was pointing at.

"You're right," Bobby said, "not an island."

It was an aircraft carrier, the deck bristling with planes and a smattering of crew members carrying out their usual duties. A massive "75" was painted on the upright portion of the ship.

Oscar shook his head. "Harry, baby, it is good to see you." He pointed and said, "Beth and Bobby, I'd like to introduce you to the USS Harry S Truman. Callsign, 'Lone Warrior.' I spent 16 months aboard…best time of my life." He was still shouting over the helicopter racket, but Beth and Bobby were surprised to see tears running down his cheeks. "But today is pretty good as well."

WHAT'S NEXT

"THIS IS STRANGE," OSCAR SAID.

"Strange doesn't come close to covering today," Beth said.

They were sitting on the deck, leaning against the gray-painted steel of the island, just trying to stay out of the way until someone came to collect them. An armed sailor kept his eye on them, without being overtly threatening.

"No," Oscar said, "I realize today is about a 14 on the Weird-Shit-O-Meter, with the previous winner being the Viking ship in Fargo, but what I'm saying is, this ship is all wrong. It's a carrier, right, a supercarrier. It should have about sixty F-18s, a few helicopters, and a smattering of other planes. This flight deck is super crowded and there's a weird assortment of planes—helicopters, Ospreys, all sorts of stuff that doesn't really belong. Plus, it's alone. Carriers are never alone—there should be a cruiser, a couple destroyers, and some supply ships. And what they're doing in Hudson Bay is just bonkers."

"Maybe the captain will tell us what's going on," Beth said.

Oscar snorted, "We're not going to talk to the captain. You need to understand, that guy is responsible for thousands of lives and billions of dollars in equipment, not to mention he might have nuclear weapons on board. We're not important at all. They dragged us out of the ocean just because it was good practice for the helo guys. Nobody on this ship is going to tell us anything or cares about us at all."

"Gunny?" a voice said.

Oscar looked around, leaped to his feet, and started to salute. "Major," then after a quick look at the uniform corrected himself, "Colonel. Good to see you, sir."

Bobby and Beth looked up to see a compact figure in a Marine uniform coming their way. He was about 5'5", maybe 130 pounds. His skin was a flat black and a long scar angled from the corner of his mouth to right above his ear.

Taking their cue from Oscar, Bobbie and Beth got to their feet. The colonel reached out his hand and shook theirs in turn.

"Hi," he said. "I'm Colonel Fisher, Bob Fisher. Gunny here and I chewed some of the same mud a few years ago."

"I've been trying to forget," Oscar said.

"How'd your hand turn out?" Colonel Fisher asked. "I lost track of you after you went to Landstuhl and I went to Walter Reed."

"Pretty good," Oscar said, holding up the mangled extremity. "They took one of my big toes and made a thumb, so it works a lot better than we thought it would."

The colonel shrugged. "I thought it worked pretty well when you were carrying me over your shoulder. It was so dark, I never did see how much it was bleeding. You know, I never could get those clothes clean—had to throw them away."

"Yeah, sucks to be you. Next time you get shot, I'll try not to be in the area," Oscar said. "What the hell are you doing here, sir?"

"I think I'm probably going to be asking you the same thing. How about I buy you a cup of coffee?"

A half hour later they were deep in the bowels of the carrier. Beth had lost track of the steel doors they'd gone through and the gray passageways. Now they were in a wood-paneled room with large round tables covered with blue tablecloths. A steward had brought repeated pots of coffee along with an assortment of pastries.

"That is the strangest story I've ever heard," Colonel Fisher said. "Dr. Hendrickson, you've certainly put your money where your mouth is, coming on this…endeavor."

Beth laughed out loud. "Colonel, please don't tell me how many words ran through your mind before you came up with 'endeavor.' Personally, I vary between 'doomed crusade' and 'what the hell were they thinking.'"

"We've had a lot of that lately."

"What's the deal, sir?" Oscar asked. "That's no Marine Air Wing up there."

"No, it's not," Colonel Fisher said. "It's what we could round up from a half dozen small deployed units. When everything went to shit, the carrier task force was in the Adriatic. They got their last orders out of Washington, which was to bring everybody home. They gathered up some troops from Croatia and Albania, including my unit, then picked up everyone we had in Tunisia and Algeria. No American troops left in the Mediterranean at all. Came with the task force back to Norfolk and Norfolk wasn't there anymore. At least, nothing useful was left—no way to refuel for the rest of the task force. We left them all there, along with a lot of the crew and the troops we'd picked up, and then…just kept going north, seeing what things looked like."

"What do they look like?" Bobby asked.

"Looks like shit. Hell of a lot of people lived on the East Coast, and most of them are gone, gone, gone. New York, Boston you could see were on fire. We've done some recon flights and the other cities don't look any better. We stopped getting orders a long time ago. By the time we got to Maine, I think the captain thought, 'What the hell, let's try the Northwest Passage. We got thirty years' worth of fuel for the reactors.' I think the plan is to end up in San Diego and see what's there."

"I might have a better idea," Bobby said.

"Was it your idea to get chased by a polar bear on your way to the North Pole? 'Cause, I'm not certain I want to take an idea like that to the captain."

Bobby said, "No, that's all on Oscar—you know what a crazy shit he is."

The colonel laughed and then turned toward Oscar. "Gunny," he said, "We've known each other a long time. I've never known you to do anything stupid. Do you really believe this trip makes sense, or are you just in it for the shits and giggles?"

Oscar shrugged helplessly. "Colonel, I don't know. You have no idea how much I didn't want to do this, how much I didn't want *anyone* to do this. But I believe—I truly believe—we are in deep shit. I can't do anything about LA or Miami. But there are millions of people who don't have to die if we pull this off. That's what I think."

Bobby leaned in. "Colonel , you took an oath. 'All enemies foreign and domestic…' something like that. I imagine you were thinking the Taliban or Russia or China. I don't know what you were thinking when you took the oath—all I know is that you did. But here you go. This is your chance, this is the best chance of everyone on this ship, to make a difference, to make a life for millions and millions of people, to start rebuilding this country, and making it safe and secure for children and for babies yet unborn. Seriously, Colonel, you have a chance to do more for more people than anyone since Chesty Puller. You haven't done anything that mattered for a year. This will take a month, a month tops, and in that time, you can change the world, Colonel. Shit, save the world." Bobby tapped the table for emphasis. "If you say 'No,' we'll get dropped off at some Eskimo village and you'll sail over the horizon and spend however long your life lasts wondering what if you were wrong."

Colonel Fisher looked at him, looked at all of them and said, "I'll take it to the captain. Have some more coffee—you're going to want to be sharp."

He left the wardroom, and Oscar took a deep breath.

Beth looked at Oscar, then she looked at Bobbie as if she were seeing something very new indeed.

“I know about Oscar,” she said, “but are you gay?”

“No.”

“Good,” she said, and grabbed him by the shirt and kissed him hard, on the mouth.

NEXT

JOHN WAS WORKING IN THE GARDEN, relishing being outside instead of stuck in the greenhouse.

He saw the man coming from a long way off. He was used to seeing people on foot, but the flood of refugees had slowed to a trickle during the winter, and he hadn't seen a stranger in a month or more.

He bent over his coat, which he'd hung on the wheelbarrow, and pulled a pistol out of a pocket, sticking it in the small of his back.

When the man came close enough, he looked vaguely familiar, although he also looked like he'd been through hell and seen more than he wanted on the trip.

John was getting used to that look.

"John?" the man asked. "Is that you?"

"Yeah. I'm sorry, you seem familiar, but I just can't place you."

"Steve, Steve Swenson. I was just at my aunt's old place, and I saw the sign you put there—that my family was here. Are they okay?"

John opened his mouth, then closed it again. "Steve, the short answer is, yes, they're fine. But it's kind of a long story. We better go in the house and have some lunch. You really look like hell."

He picked up his coat and motioned for Steve to go ahead of him. They were halfway to the house when Abby came around the corner and looked up. She paused, looked again, and then screamed, "DADDY!"

John watched the tearful reunion, basking in the warmth of their emotion, but then took a deep breath.

There was a lot to talk about.

TO BE CONTINUED...

www.ingramcontent.com/pod-product-compliance
Lightning Source LLC
Chambersburg PA
CBHW060444310726

48977CB00001B/315